The Soulful Seeker

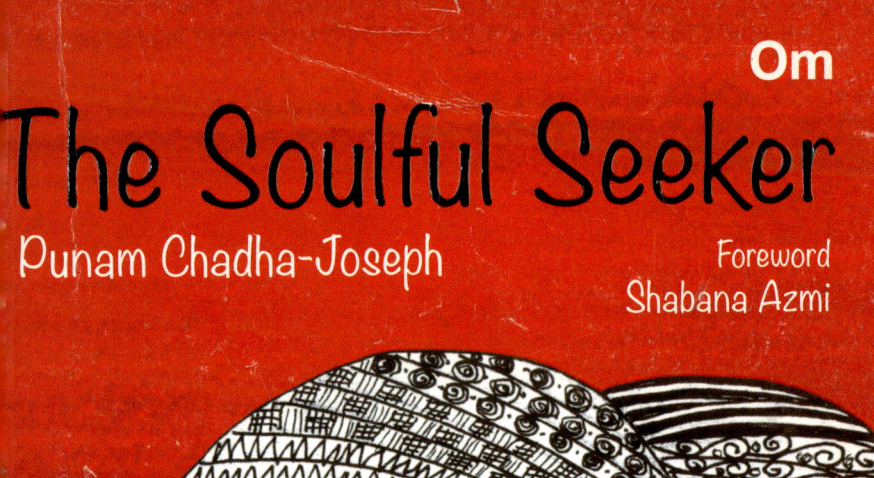

Punam Chadha-Joseph

Foreword
Shabana Azmi

Om

After completing her Bachelor's in Economics (Honours) from St. Xavier's College, Mumbai, Punam Chadha-Joseph joined the prestigious Oberoi School of Hotel Management in Delhi to do her post-graduation. This was followed by a 5-year stint in Food and Beverage and Sales and Marketing at the Hotel Oberoi Towers in Mumbai.

Her journey then took her to the world of Advertising in Account Management, where she spent several years with top agencies like Lintas and Mudra, spearheading campaigns for many prestigious brands.

In the course of her work-life, she met her husband Sabbas Joseph, the Founder-Director of Wizcraft, India's pioneer Event Management agency. She is the mother of a 21-year-old son Rohan, and a 17-year-old daughter Rhea, both of whom are currently pursuing their academic careers.

Punam is a lover of the arts and has also tried her hand at a successful business of artifacts, called 'Artifactors'. Her other passions include reading, writing poetry, travelling, hand-crafting jewellery and sewing.

While her travels have taken her to many different and exotic parts of the world, she continues to live and enjoy her life in Mumbai. Her poems however reflect thoughts and emotions that are universal in nature and can appeal to readers across the globe.

The Soulful Seeker is her first book of poems, and she is ready with another one, especially written for children, based on appreciating and saving the environment.

Sketching being a new hobby, she has incorporated many of her sketches in *The Soulful Seeker*, including the very striking visual on the cover.

The Soulful Seeker
Punam Chadha-Joseph

Foreword
Shabana Azmi

Om Books International

First published in 2016 by

Om Books International

Corporate & Editorial Office
A-12, Sector 64, Noida 201 301
Uttar Pradesh, India
Phone: +91 120 477 4100
Email: editorial@ombooks.com
Website: www.ombooksinternational.com

Sales Office
107, Ansari Road, Darya Ganj
New Delhi 110 002, India
Phone: +91 11 4000 9000
Fax: +91 11 2327 8091
Email: sales@ombooks.com
Website: www.ombooks.com

Text & Illustrations copyright © Punam Chadha-Joseph 2016

ALL RIGHTS RESERVED. No part of this book may be reproduced or transmitted in any form by any means, electronic or mechanical, including photocopying and recording, or by any information storage and retrieval system, except as may be expressly permitted in writing by the publisher.

ISBN: 978-93-84625-43-6

Printed in India

10 9 8 7 6 5 4 3 2 1

For

My parents Rajni and Mohindra Chadha,
My husband Sabbas Joseph,
And my children Rohan and Rhea.

Love you all forever ...

Sometimes lost, sometimes found,
Sometimes silly, sometimes sound,
Sometimes straight, sometimes round ...
Oh, the circle of Life ... ever so profound!

Contents

Foreword: Shabana Azmi

1 Soul & Self — 19

Waiting to Exhale	20
Growing Old	21
Am I Dead?	22
Setting Myself Free	24
Life!	26
Verse or Curse?	27
Ageing	28
Between the Lines	31
Just Happy to be Me	32
The Journey	34
Thoughts	36
The New Me	38
Do I Matter?	40
Alike	42
Giving Wings	43
The Power of Perfection	44
Spoken Words	45
Arguments	46
All Knotted Up	48
The Eternal Quest	50
Being Tough	51
I Write	52
My World	55
The Equation	56
The Race	57

2 Love & Longing — 59

- I Have a Need — 60
- A 'State of Being' — 62
- Love — 64
- What is Love? — 66
- Companionship — 68
- They Say, I Say — 69
- My Imperfect Heart — 70
- Celebrations — 72
- First Love — 74
- Just Words — 76

3 Family & Friends — 79

- Mother's Day — 80
- Saturday Night — 82
- A Son Turns 20 — 84
- On My Husband's Birthday — 85
- The Reunion — 86
- Memories — 88
- A Son's 15th Birthday — 89
- A Son's 17th Birthday — 90
- Wrapped Around — 91
- My Daughter and Her Tattoo — 92
- On Meeting an Old Friend — 94
- School Friends' Reunion — 96
- For a Daughter's 17th Birthday — 97
- Forever a Child — 98
- Birthday Poem for a Father — 100
- My Children — 102
- On Friendship — 104

4 Fears & Frustrations — 107

Demons — 108
The Future? — 109
Snakes in the Grass — 110
Conversations in My Head — 111
Beware! — 112
How Will it End? — 114
Exams! — 116
Being Vocal — 118
It's War! — 119

5 Happiness & Hope — 121

Ode to an Educator — 122
The Obstacle Race — 125
Happy? — 126
Bonding — 128
Living in the Present — 130
What is Happiness? — 132
My Friend's Garden — 133
On Happiness — 134
The Sum Total — 136
When Should I Stop Dreaming? — 137
Sweet 16 — 138
Soaring — 139

6 Despondency & Despair — 141

Let's Rise — 142
Should I Worry? — 146
Delusion — 148
Chores — 150
The Clouds and the Carcass — 152

7	**Ache & Acceptance**	**155**
	In Appreciation	156
	A Farewell to Breasts	159
	The Addiction	160
	The Old Nightie	162
	Chasing Unicorns	164
	From Me to You … and Back?	166
	Past, Present and Future	168
	Life, a Puzzle	170
	Carpe Diem	171
	A Dash	172
	Don't Forget to Care	174
	The Open Book	176
	Nip and Tuck	178
	The New Normal	179
	Cleaning My Room	180
	Momentum	182
	The Memory Box	184
	The Idealist	186
8	**Questions & Queries**	**189**
	Still Thinking	190
	Misfits	192
	The Drama That is Life!	194
	Game of Chance	196
	The Two Devils	198
	Distinct or Not?	200
	Thoughts	202
	My Mind	204
	Time	206

9	**Benevolence & Belief**	**209**
	Simple Joys and Simpler Pleasures	210
	Reality	212
	Being Bold	214
	The Parallel Universe	216
	The 'Splinter'	218
	What's in a Name?	220
	Blind Faith	222
	Life Can be Extreme	224
	The Decreasing 10	225
10	**Dreams & Desires**	**227**
	The Illusion	228
	Sometimes	230
	Expectations	231
	My Diamond	232
	Between a Rock and a Very Hard Place	234
	The Dragon	237
	In the Mood for Food	238
	The Exercise Plan	240
	Random Thoughts	243
11	**Frivolous & Fun**	**245**
	Tommy the Cat	246
	Mosquito, Mosquito	248
Acknowledgments		251

Foreword

It has been famously said that poetry is 'felt thought'. It is an interesting paradox that poetry is defined by words but needs to transcend words if it is to be truly meaningful.

In an increasingly market-driven world, the Fine Arts take a hit because their impact is not immediately evident. But as celebrated Urdu poet Javed Akhtar says, "Poetry is not an aspirin which you pop to make the headache disappear instantly. Instead, it is like a vitamin that slowly strengthens your aesthetic muscles and nourishes you with inner beauty."

It is this quest for inner beauty that we find in Punam's maiden book of poetry *The Soulful Seeker*.

It is a matter of concern that women's voices have not earned the visibility they deserve because in Indian society particularly, tales our grandmothers told us came from a culture of oral tradition in which women's voices were seldom recorded. That is why we need a sustained effort to provide the space for their experiences to be mainstreamed.

Punam grew up in a home filled with academics, books and learning. Early exposure to the arts – music, painting, dance, poetry and evenings spent in the company of various artists, who were her parents' friends, resulted in a passionate interest in art and culture.

However, the challenges of getting married, building a home and being a devoted mother to her two children, left her with little time to pursue her passion.

Fortunately, the advent of technology and the Internet, particularly the email, resulted in her connecting with her close group of school friends from across the world. As they shared their lives on a daily basis, via long emails, Punam discovered that she often wrote/replied in rhyme. It came quite naturally to her and encouraged by her friends and family, she began writing poetry.

The Soulful Seeker, is a collection of her thoughts, emotions and feelings, written over a period of time. Triggered by a word, a sentence, an object or even an emotion, Punam has effectively captured sentiments common to us all.

The poems resonate with tremendous honesty and even occasional despair. While some poems are light and joyful, the more intense and soul-searching ones show the range of her concerns. And like a true artist, she mines her personal experiences and boldly shares and exposes her internal conflicts and angst. But through it all, there is a very positive message of acceptance and a constant yearning for achieving her dreams and desires ... Each reader will undoubtedly identify with many of the poems.

Interestingly, all the illustrations in the book including the cover, have also been done by Punam – the artist in her, buried for some time in household duties has been resurrected. Hopefully she will continue on her artistic journey.

Shabana Azmi
Mumbai
January 2016

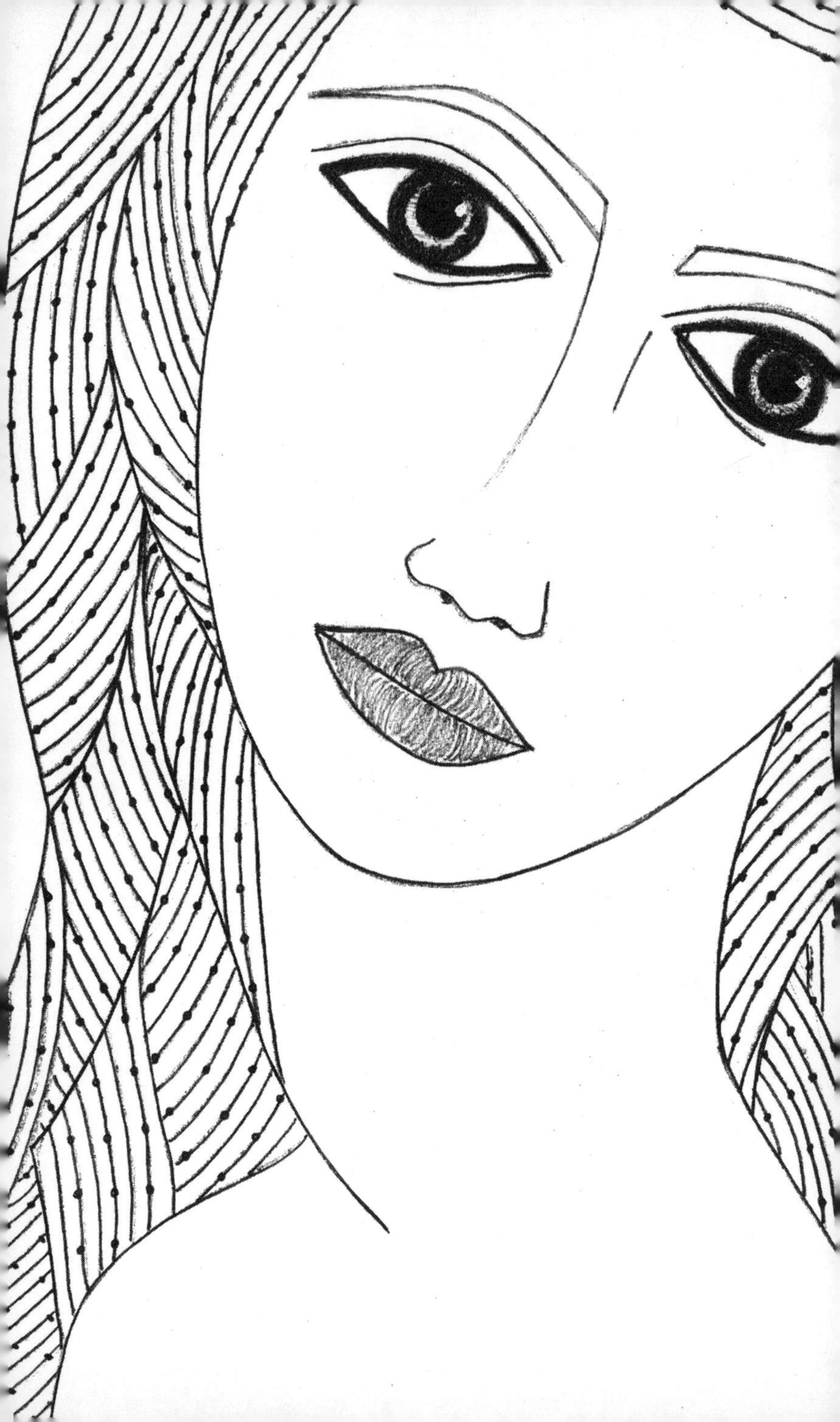

1

Soul & Self

Waiting to Exhale

Ever get the feeling that a bee's stuck in your head?
A thought that just keeps buzzing, filling you with dread?

There really isn't any reason for this feeling to be there.
Surely there's something, that my subconscious wants to share.

We all have our dark secrets, terrible anxieties and fears,
some inherent to our nature, some acquired over the years.

I know I fight my demons, that within me latent lie.
Oh, but they can be wicked, and often don't comply.

The buzzing's getting louder, it's invading my very soul.
My heart's beating faster, I think I'm losing control.

The feeling's so overpowering, to the pit of my stomach it goes.
A strong vice-like grip, it has me in its throes.

But I know that I'm strong, I'll fight it off bit by bit.
Just watch as I regain control, I'm not the one to quit.

How can I let a little buzzing just snatch away my joy?
There's so much to be grateful for, and so much to enjoy.

So, though I secretly dread what the future will entail,
For now, I'm just waiting, just waiting to exhale.

Growing Old

Ever since I've turned 40, I've had a strange preoccupation –
thoughts of self-preservation – I'm definitely on a mission!
I read every article written on the subject
of how to become the most desirable object.

Ladies, take no offence, don't object to such a deed.
We all strive to be wanted, it's an inherent human need.
Before going to a party, I change my clothes but thrice,
to look my slimmest best, or, at least to look just nice.

When I look around, and see women young and tall,
I walk a little straighter, trying hard to give it my all.
Do I really need to compete? I wonder in my head.
Answers clutter my mind but I leave them all unsaid.

And if I happen to see by even a remote chance,
a male in the room, casting an admiring glance,
I turn on the charm, with oh, so much ease.
It's second nature to me, I hope you understand, please.

With supreme confidence, on many subjects I speak.
I'm truly in my element, I'm really at my peak.
And as men flock to me, with attention so kind,
it's less for my body and more for my 'beautiful' mind.

So, while the years have, on my body taken their toll,
adding a mesh of wisdom lines, I'm still on a roll.
With age comes experience that time cannot stop.
So what if I no longer fit into that sexy tank top?

Am I Dead?

Am I dead? I wondered as I got out of bed.
Why was my mind so empty, no thoughts in my head?
Maybe I was dreaming, I really couldn't be sure.
Then why was there another me, standing by the door?

Was I but a body, with just another soul?
Was the one by the door, actually a ghoul?
I stared at it, it stared right back.
Should I seriously be scared of that maniac?

But if it's me, then I know me well.
So in two bodies, how can I dwell?
Which one's real? I'm scared to guess.
Someone help me. I'm in a mess.

It continued to stare with a vacant gaze.
Was it real? I'm still in a daze.
For surely in Life, there's more to me,
than this apparition that only I can see?

I'm definitely dead – that was now my conviction,
for I'm sure in Life, I had caused a little friction,
with a heart that beat, and a body that bled,
with love to give, and happiness to spread.

Then how did I become one by two?
If I am me, then who are you?
Are you my dream that is dying first,
or just a nightmare – one of the worst?

I think I'm caught in a deep dark well.
Clearly, this has to be my personal hell.
Awake, asleep or really dead?
I think I'm just going back to bed.

Setting Myself Free

Like a moth to a flame, I'm often drawn.
Between spontaneity and safe, I'm sometimes torn.
A feeling of excitement, with every new dawn,
usually elated am I, though at times rather forlorn.

A spring in my step, a shiver down my spine,
dare I cross, the forbidden line?
Do I decide for myself, or wait for a sign,
bow to expectations, or embrace what's mine?

Life is a paradox, of feelings high and low,
a raging of emotions, from super-fast to slow.
On days, I light up, have a perpetual glow,
on others, I slip back, just go with the flow.

My friends call me 'sunshine', so dare I disclose,
the dark shadows lurking from my head to my toes.
I put up a brave front, holding my insecurities close.
Is my happy face a reality, or just another pose?

Sometimes, I project a persona, where I'm at my best.
At other times, I simply put all my feelings to rest.
I feel like I'm on a never-ending quest,
constantly putting my emotions, to some kind of test.

Each day, along with joy, does also sorrow bring.
Despite all hope, there's no eternal Spring.
Yet, I continue to wait, do the expected thing.
Aren't we all bound together by an invisible string?

We all have a face, a veritable mask.
'Must I always hide behind it?' I do dare ask.
Being happy is not easy, it's an uphill task.
Yet, in my sunshine, may my dear ones bask.

Substance over superficiality, is a choice I must make,
if not for myself, at least, for my loved ones' sake.
From inner demons and fears, for once let my soul awake.
Yes, I'm finally giving myself, a much-needed break.

I'll start by being grateful, for all that's been given to me.
Little bubbles of happiness, that I often forget to see,
the vastness of the universe, from the sky to the sea.
Yes, I'm finally setting myself, setting myself free.

Life!

Some days I write for pleasure, some days I write in pain.
Either way it's a catharsis, from which I can only gain.

And as I let flow my emotions, whatever they might be,
I know I'm exposing my inner angst, for everyone to see.

It's not an easy task, to verbalise what I feel –
the ideas, thoughts, concerns, and problems with which I deal.

My writing reflects what I feel,
as I live through each day,
and this unburdening of my inner being,
sometimes even shows me the way.

To re-chart the journey of my Life and reinvent myself,
for if from my mistakes I do not learn, it's a disservice to myself.

'Change is the only constant',
is a phrase that's often used.
Staying frozen in time,
not moving on, can no longer be excused.

With age comes experience and a wad of wisdom too.
How much of it I internalise, is totally within my purview.

So, as I continue to challenge myself
And give my thoughts a voice,
I know it's a decision that I have made,
It's entirely my own choice.

Yes, I'd like to constantly evolve, yet not lose my very essence,
for a Life not lived, true to oneself, is a Life of mere pretence!

Verse or Curse?

I like to write and I like to write in verse,
though sometimes I wonder, if it's actually a curse.
I put down my thoughts and they're usually set in rhyme,
silly, banal, profound, and sometimes even sublime.

So I often walk around, with an expression of daze,
as my mind constantly searches, for that perfect phrase.
Sometimes I even worry, that when I say things aloud,
it sounds like a recitation, in front of a disinterested crowd.

But what can I do, if in rhyme I do think,
putting pen to paper before I lose the link?

The problem with this curse is, that it's often at its best,
at a time when my body, I'm about to put down to rest.
If that's not bad enough, it's in the middle of a shower,
that I'm bombarded with thoughts, of a higher power.

And as I rush out, trying not to slip on the floor,
To save these profound words and some more,

I find that I've suddenly,
drawn a complete blank,
and there's nothing more flowing out,
of the usually active think-tank!

That's how sometimes, I lose a precious gem.
It's definitely a curse of perpetual mayhem.

Ageing

When I was 14, 40 seemed a million miles away.
At 15, 50 was still somewhere in the Milky Way.
Yet, today, those very landmarks as I've begun to cross,
a new reality emerges, ageing is the new ethos.

I'm reading an article on ageing
and how I'm growing old.
Should I continue with this reading,
or just put it on hold?
Will it make me feel older,
as I relate to what's being told,
even though in my head,
I still feel so young and bold?

I belong to a generation,
that has seen many an innovation –
from computer hardware,
to complex smartphone creation.
Through conflicts with my kids,
over their choices and ambitions,
I run the race of Life,
with a bundle of contradictions.

From being the youngest in the room,
now I'm at times the oldest around,
accepting the brilliance of today's youth,
as they boldly stand their ground.
It's not an easy reality to accept,
since mentally I'm still so sound.

Yet, their new theories, I must admit,
often leave me quite spellbound.

Untimely deaths, uncertain health
and occasional memory loss,
reinforce the fact, that I'm past my prime,
I'm no longer the boss.
And while coloured hair and body care
can occasionally add some gloss,
the truth is that I'm obsolete,
maybe even an object of pathos!

I thought I belonged to a generation,
that just would never age.
Tricked into wrongly believing this,
sure puts me in a rage.
With every group of young people,
I'm constantly trying to gauge,
if my youthful appearance and demeanour,
put me on the same page.

This undesirable quandary makes me unhappy,
since I'm no longer cutting-edge.
How soon have I lost my importance,
a fall from my lofty ledge.
The reality of age and obsolescence,
has created a sharp wedge.
My confidence and self-esteem have fallen,
is also what they allege.

With youth came excitement,
a feeling of empowerment,
the ability to decide, do,
and my constant advancement.
Decisions were based,
on the accuracy of my judgement.
I usually called the shots
and juggled many an adjustment.

Yet, the time has come,
to give up this revered crown,
as the youngsters question me
with a disapproving frown.
It's not easy to be strong,
as my world turns upside down.
I must channelise my energies elsewhere,
to avoid a breakdown.

So as the circle of Life,
keeps spinning without a stop,
my role I must reconsider,
don't want to be a mere prop.
And as I accept the challenge,
and from the mainstream do drop,
I know my experience and wisdom,
they'll soon want to co-opt.

Between the Lines

The lines on my forehead, have many a story to tell.
Should I read between the lines, and on them dwell?
Or should I just pretend, that they're barely there,
and not worry too much about the how and where?

But when in the mirror, I see them staring back at me,
I know I can't ignore the stories, behind what I see.
And though Life has dealt me, a hand better than most,
I have my own troubles, and my own internal ghost.

Each frown of the brow, holds within its depth,
feelings and emotions, which into my Life have crept.
Though wish them away, I try with my might,
with destiny and fate, I really can't fight.

And so I embrace them, as a part of who I am.
No Botox for me, can't be a part of that sham.
And if age and experience, do my lines increase,
I'll be proud of the stories, hidden within each crease.

Now when I see them, they bring memories to the fore,
of a Life well lived, of experiences galore,
of days gone by, and the joys and whines.
Yes, it's so cathartic, to read between the lines.

Just Happy to be Me

Is it a crime to like oneself?
I sat and wondered aloud.
Does it make me terribly conceited,
or maybe just a wee bit proud?

I know that I have several flaws,
and more than an obvious imperfection.
So does that mean that of myself,
I actually have a wrong perception?

I pondered over this for many a day,
and had a serious debate with myself.
And as I looked at who I am,
the answer came by itself.

It's not what I am that makes me
the person whom I like,
but who I am and what I do,
that gives me that extra strike.

I say what I mean and mean what I say,
and to my word remain true.
I battle the odds, go out on a limb
to ensure that I see things through.

I like to take that extra step
to create a comfort zone,
in person if I possibly can,
or at least, by a buzz on the phone.

Since Life is short, I do my best
to spread some happiness around.
So having done my best all through the day,
I ensure that my sleep is sound.

This is no boast, I don't mean to brag,
I'm just giving myself a boost.
Since no one else pats my back,
for myself, all this I've deduced.

And before someone refutes my claims,
and myself I begin to doubt,
I must confess, it's not easy to like
oneself all day, in and out.

But since I know who I am,
and l like what I see,
I tell myself, objections or not,
I'm just happy to be me!

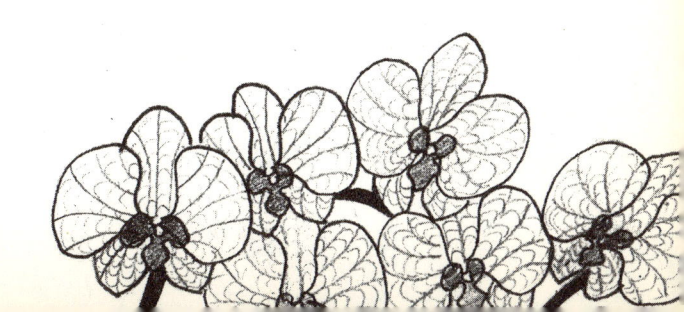

The Journey

Is Life about ambition, success
and a legacy to leave behind,
or just the pursuit of happiness
through any means I can find?

Can I only be happy
if I make a strong impact?
Why does doing nothing 'useful'
make others adversely react?

So what if I once led a team,
that often raised a storm,
burning the midnight oil,
doing tasks that made me strong.

Through conflicts and struggles,
the ongoing desire to find
that which made an impact,
through means, at times unkind.

Why can't I be happy,
in just a simple way,
count all my blessings
and experiences each day?

Why do I feel the need,
to make a statement in my Life,
the heady feeling of power,
achieved not without strife?

Where has it led me?
Am I in a happy place?
Or have I just thoughtlessly run,
in Life's mindless race?

I've faced the risks that come,
with trust, intimacy and sharing.
Does that mean that I must now,
give up and just stop caring?

I hang on to what I feel
I just can't do without.
But in reality I need so little,
of that there is no doubt.

And yet the search is eternally on,
as I keep hoping to find,
that which makes my Life count –
the obvious and the undefined.

So in my pursuit of happiness,
I must continue to face,
the travails of living,
before I'm gone without a trace.

For wherever I go,
I must take myself with me.
Slow and steady, fast and furious,
Who knows what I'm meant to be.

Thoughts

My mind flits like a butterfly,
from thought to thought and more,
looking to settle on the one,
that I've never explored before.

What gives rise to thoughts?
Is it the experiences of each day?
Or just mundane activities,
as I react to what's in my way.

Are thoughts like beautiful flowers,
that attract the butterfly and the bee?
Or are they like a spider's web
that entraps the fly and the flea?

Then how do I decide,
which one to latch on to?
Both are alluring in their way.
It's all about a point of view.

Some thoughts help me rise,
and determine what I do,
while others pull me down,
and turn my reactions askew.

Yet I know that I can't decide,
which one takes the lead.
It's finally all a matter of what,
my subconscious wants to heed.

So as I let my mind continue,
to flit from thought to thought,
I'm happy in the realisation,
that thoughtless at least I'm not.

The New Me

I want to reinvent myself,
become the person I'm meant to be.
But how do I determine who that is?
Can I rely merely on what others see?

I think I know myself,
yet, my own analysis I do doubt.
Am I the happy person with a smile,
or the one with a perpetual pout?

Am I the one I dream about,
In colour, and black and white,
or am I the one who others see,
with no inkling of my inner plight?

In my mind and in my head,
I stand powerful and tall.
Yet in the presence of learned ones,
I feel insignificant and small.

Am I stuck in the same old routine,
in the sameness of all things?
Same conversation, same position,
with nothing new to give me wings?

I dream the impossible dream,
which while awake, I cannot see.
So who am I? What makes me tick?
Who after all is the real me?

Am I the title that I have,
or the work that I daily do?
Am I the trimmings that I have?
Really don't know what to view.

Yet as I continue this race,
against age, time and fears,
I know I have to take the leap,
before I run out of years.

So each day I teach myself,
a new thing or even two,
So glad am I to keep learning,
as a brand new me, I pursue.

Do I Matter?

Sometimes I wonder when my day is done,
will I be remembered as a special one,
or just a being who lived her Life,
as a daughter, mother and even a wife?

Has my Life meant anything at all,
to those around me and some on call,
or have I just many roles played,
sometimes bold, yet often afraid?

Has there been a purpose to my Life,
meaningful at all, or just futile strife?
Have I been able to leave behind a mark?
A gentle shadow or one that's stark?

Is my destiny the one I chose to make,
or predetermined for me to just partake?
Have I been for some greatness born?
And when I go, will anyone mourn?

Will an edifice be built in my name,
a candle lit or an eternal flame?
What are the deeds that'll make me great?
What should I do? What should I create?

Aren't the roles that I play in Life enough,
with daily challenges, some very tough?
Juggling and struggling to get through each day,
without harming anyone, even leading the way?

Maybe each small action will have a ripple effect.
One that I don't know of right now or even suspect.
Sometimes I believe we forget our true worth,
our importance to some, since the time of our birth.

So maybe I don't need to especially try
to be remembered after the final goodbye.
For if I've lived a Life honest and true,
I'll be happy to have mattered to even a few!

Alike

I have so many eccentricities that set me apart,
making me who I am and that's the best part.
Just as I can't be you, you too can't be me.
Even if we think alike, we're as different as can be.

Of course there are days when I wish I could be you,
hoping that sometimes you'd want to be me too.
And even if we are almost an extension of each one,
my quirks are so unique to me, that me you can't become.

Some traits I was born with, some came along the way,
emotions and experiences that changed me day by day.
So even if I wish that I could be more like you,
my own circumstances have made me special too.

And while there are days when I just don't want to be me,
a kind word from someone can miraculously set me free.
So while I hope to imbibe what about you I do like,
I've interestingly just realised that we're not so unlike.

Giving Wings

Today I've decided to give my mind wings,
untie it from all its tightly-knotted strings.
Letting it lose thus, may well land me in a mess,
but where else it could lead me, is anyone's guess.

Try as I might so often to set myself free,
I'm fearful, to cross the pre-set boundary.
For if given wings to rise above and soar,
I might find myself in the unknown and obscure.

And maybe it's this risk that keeps me contained,
with my thoughts and desires subconsciously chained.
Would I dare dance nude when the first rains come,
or have thoughts that many may find worrisome?

I have truly longed to do as I please,
break out of my shackles, get a swift release.
And although nothing or nobody is holding me back,
don't want for my behaviour, to be branded a maniac.

For in this world, we are each allotted a place,
a sphere within which to function, a finite space.
The few who dare this invisible line cross,
often end up in a Life of despair and pathos.

And sadly, it's only when they are reduced to dust,
that the world acknowledges that it was really quite unjust.
And as these thoughts and more, keep debating in my mind,
my outstretched wings, once again, I've decided to bind.

The Power of Perfection

The pursuit of perfection can be an intimidating thought,
often leading to procrastination, and resulting in nought.

I too seek excellence, then get discouraged along the way,
paralysed into defeat, when I'm not even mid-way.

The goals that I set for myself are long and far,
from the bold and beautiful to the simple and bizarre.

The hurdles along the way can be a deterring force.
Can I last long enough to stay this demanding course?

They say the most difficult is the very first step,
the most challenging one, for which you really must prep.

But if I can break my goals into chunks that can be achieved,
they might be less daunting than what I'd initially perceived.

And if it's perfection that I want, I'll have to give it my best.
I must relentlessly trudge on, with little or no time to rest.

For nothing of significance can be achieved unless
it's built slowly and surely, so I must strive on regardless.

And as I brace myself to march valiantly ahead,
each step taking me closer as I do carefully tread.

The euphoria and power of achieving near perfection,
shall hereafter be my motivation and even my redemption.

Spoken Words

Ever face that situation when the words just rush out
and you know you've said too much, without any doubt,
not knowing what led you to say what you did,
words that were harsh and maybe even acrid?

Do you wonder then if the words were meant to hurt,
a result of pent-up feelings that came out in a spurt?
Or were they misdirected, as you lost your composure,
biting your tongue now as you lament this exposure?

We are complex beings and try as we might,
our prejudices are deep-rooted, often hidden out of sight.
And that's when the smallest nudge can make us react
as we reveal our true selves, cut out the act.

Complexes and biases within each of us do exist,
superior, preconceived, narrow-minded and even sexist.
And for long periods, latent within us they do lie
till unexpectedly they leap out and we don't know why.

As humans we are cautious in what we do and say,
controlling our actions and behaviour through most of the day,
but then there comes that time and place
where we expose our true selves, as might be the case.

Then think about the words we didn't mean but said,
hoping against hope that they weren't misread.
And as we apologise profusely and try to make amends,
It's the ones who forgive us that are our true friends.

Arguments

I was talking to myself,
just the other day.
Holding forth on varied topics,
there was so much I wanted to say.

I knew if I voiced my thoughts to others,
they might elicit a smile,
but to me, myself and I,
they all sounded so worthwhile.

And as I discussed and argued,
I would have never really guessed,
the intensity with which,
my opinions I expressed.

I almost even began to like,
the sound of my own voice,
like all those television anchors,
who with their power do rejoice.

And even shut you up
as you start expressing your view,
thrusting upon you their opinions,
without letting your words get through.

And then I got confused,
amidst all this verbal crossfire,
whether it was me, myself or I
who was causing all this ire.

So as I pleaded with each one
to just try and speak in turn,
my behaviour, I realised
was becoming a cause for concern.

All Knotted Up

I know that I'm not perfect
but the question that bothers me so
is whether I'm as imperfect as others,
or are my imperfections more?

Does my being imperfect
cloud my better judgement?
Or do the imperfections of others
make me feel quite confident?

We each strive for perfection,
and try and do our best
but how can that be judged
if each is no better than the rest?

How do we define our imperfections?
From whose point of view do we see?
For the imperfections of others,
could look like perfection to me.

And which is that point
when I can safely assume,
there's no more scope for improvement,
since I'm truly the best one in the room?

And as I keep questioning
these imperfections and more,
I can see that it's a challenge
to even try and keep the score.

So maybe I'll just stop thinking
about others and their blots,
and strive to better what I can
by slowly untying my own knots.

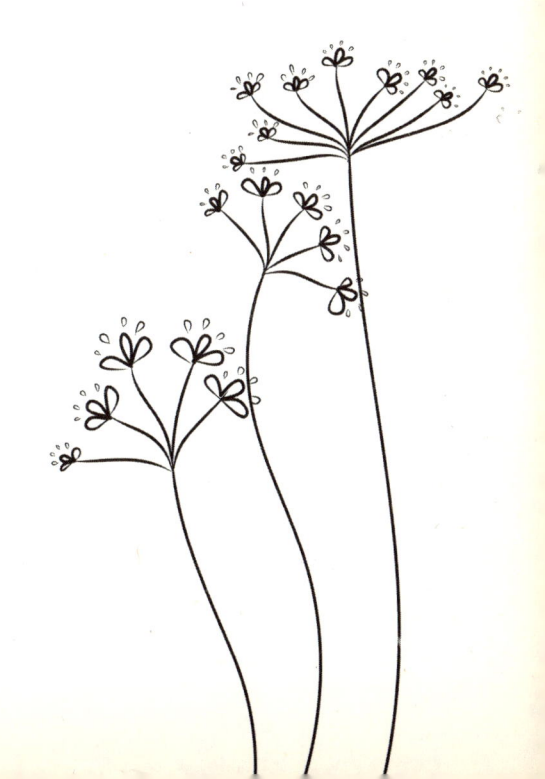

The Eternal Quest

I talk to myself all day in my head
from morning, till the time I go to bed.
Is it because my Life is mine, and mine alone?
Am I my only own friend, when I'm in this special zone?

Sometimes, I speak aloud, answering questions I dread.
Other times I just sit still, leaving many things unsaid.
Maybe, I'm just scared to shock others by my thoughts.
Don't want to be the butt of judgements and onslaughts.

Should I get out of my comfort zone and voice what I think?
What if I scare my friends away and lose that special link?
I believe that I am normal, then why do I have this fear
that my thoughts are quite crazy and my head's a bit unclear.

Family, friends and mentors in my Life all have a place.
Don't want to burden them if myself I do 'disgrace'.
I must admit though, my thoughts aren't always 'chaste',
and glad am I that their origin really can't be traced.

So, as I continue with this dialogue in my head,
I've just convinced myself, there's nothing to dread.
For each of us has these deep-seated fears,
often given vent, in the form of copious tears.

And so I say with confidence and pride,
'Think what you must, don't let others decide.
For it's you and only you, who knows you best.
So don't let anything stop your personal quest.'

Being Tough

What do you do when your heart thunders
with such a deafening sound
that you lose perspective of who you are
and even all that's around?

A buzz in your head, a blur in the eye,
a feeling so overwhelmingly strong,
leaving you wondering what it's all about,
and whether things are going right or wrong.

An emotion can arise at any time
but one as intense as this
comes only from a broken heart, a loved one gone
or the euphoria of a first kiss.

Winning a race against all odds
or even a presentation gone well
are some of the things in Life
that can with happiness make you swell.

And as the noise subsides
and you regain your composure,
depending on the inherent cause,
you limit or expand your exposure.

And as Life continues in its wake
to throw us curve balls rough,
it's how you catch them, high or low
that determines if you are tough.

I Write

I write when I am happy,
I write when I am sad,
I write when I am frustrated,
I write when I feel bad.
This would make you think
that all I do is write.
Maybe it's just my way
of gaining new insight.

I write when I am heartbroken,
I write when at a loss,
I write to vent my anger,
I write amidst chaos.
This would make you think
that all I do is write.
Maybe it's just my way
of making things all right.

I write when I am working,
I write when I am afraid,
I write when I am hurting,
I write when I have been played.
This would make you think
that all I do is write.
Maybe it's just my way
of finding my inner light.

I write when I am confused,
I write when I am weak,

I write when I am annoyed,
I write when I cannot speak.
This would make you think
that all I do is write.
Maybe it's just my way
of avoiding a fight.

I write when I am cautious,
I write when I am calm,
I write when I am impatient,
I write to do no harm.
This would make you think
that all I do is write.
Maybe it's just my way,
my thoughts, to highlight.

I write when I am gentle,
I write when I am kind,
I write when I am hopeful,
I write when in a bind.
This would make you think
that all I do is write.
Maybe it's just my way
of not being impolite.

I write when I am distracted,
I write when I am proud,
I write when I am reckless,

I write when in a crowd.
This would make you think
that all I do is write.
Maybe it's just my way
of continuing to excite.

And as I write and write,
to convey each passing notion,
glad am I to have the words
to express each fleeting emotion.

My World

For a long time now I've lived in a daze
of an alternate reality that's a perpetual haze.
My existence within it continues to amaze
and try as I might, I just can't part ways.

I view the world from within yet afar.
I am its full moon and even its rising star,
living in my personal universe, with the door slightly ajar,
tracking Life as it passes with my own radar.

I believe in myself and selfish as it may seem,
I delight in my uniqueness, my own special theme.
Some might believe that this is but a dream
but me, myself and I, we make a great team.

My own world exists in my time and space,
a deliberate attempt to opt out of the race
that the real world imposes at every pace
with threats of failure, and even disgrace.

But blessed am I to live two lives in one,
going from one to another, at times for just fun,
yet challenging myself, for a perfect union
of success and happiness before each day is done.

Bold words indeed, one might say
but we each seek a path and this is my way,
of embracing the challenges of each new day
for the world only sees what you portray.

The Equation

Are we what we think we are?
A sum of our total,
a definitive of being,
not something equivocal.

A complex equation
that defies definition.
A joining together,
of unknown contradiction.

The reflection in the mirror,
do we add or subtract?
Is it the final reality,
or just something abstract?

The passage of time,
multiplies our layers,
turning us from pawns,
into experienced players.

So we divide and rule,
to retain our power,
interpreting ourselves
to the need of the hour.

And while this paradox,
we continue to solve,
a new equation of our self,
may just happen to evolve.

The Race

If Life is a competition, who judges the race,
who signals the beginning, who determines the pace?
Do we compete with ourselves, in a predetermined space,
or keep reinventing the rules, as we change our base?

Even our birth, is a race of a kind,
as we burst into the world, after months of being confined.
And slowly in Life, our roles get defined,
as in the busyness of living, we get entwined.

Where have we come from, and where will we go?
It's anybody's guess, so we go with the flow.
There's so much to learn, and so much to know
as we live with the hope, of another tomorrow.

We compete with each other, to stay a pace ahead,
charting a sinuous path, and a road to tread.
But the passage of time, we continue to dread.
Will we have won the race, before we're dead?

So can we, if at all, bow out of this race?
Would not competing at all, lead us to disgrace?
If it's only ourselves, that we finally have to face,
we might as well live, with dignity and grace.

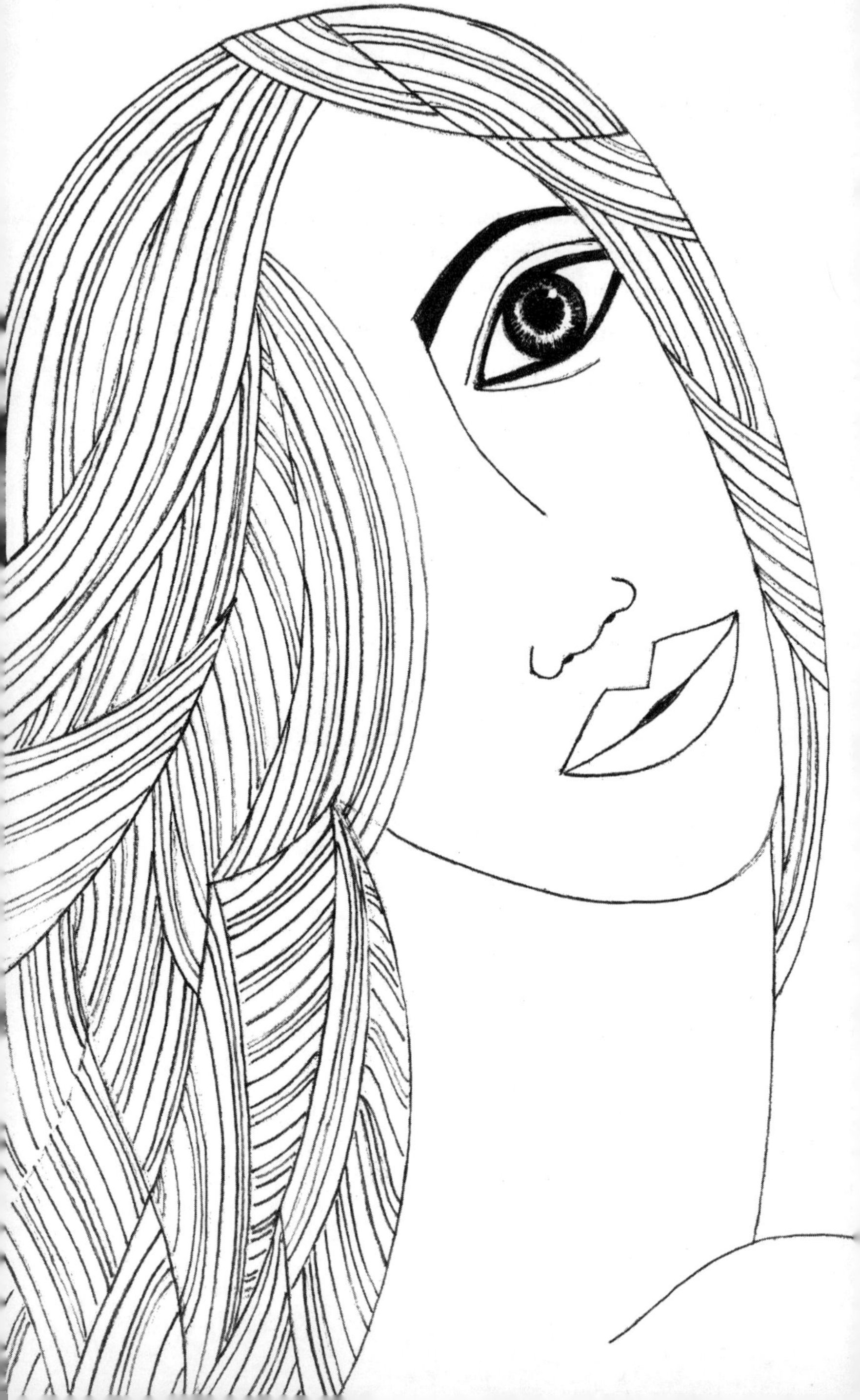

2

Love & Longing

I Have a Need

I have a need to be needed,
and it's not just a passing phase.
For a while, I thought it was no more
than just a simple craze.

But then, as time went by,
I realised this need was here to stay.
It's what relationships are based on,
and what keeps me from going astray.

I convince myself that I need
to love and be loved in return.
Then I turn all possessive and clingy,
and let jealousy within me burn.

For if I need another,
then him I need to trust.
So why do I restrain my feelings,
and unspoken, let them rust?

That then is the irony
of thought, word and deed.
There never is a right time
to let the perfect ones breed.

Each time I allow myself
to let down my guard,
it turns out to be the instance
that leaves me hurt and scarred.

Yet somewhere within me,
there continues to be hope
that someone needs me as much
so I shouldn't needlessly mope.

And as I love unconditionally,
one day I hope to redeem,
the feelings that collide with another's,
who's living the same dream.

A 'State of Being'

If love is, as they say, 'a state of being'
then what is it that I'm just not seeing?
For if I'm happy, then why does love make me sad,
and which are those times when for love I'm glad?

If love turns an adult into a child,
with emotions ranging from severe to mild,
then why is it that I can no longer admire
the one who was once the object of my desire?

If love is that which brought us close,
why then is it now a game of innuendos?
What state of being makes us toil
to arouse such conflict and obsessive turmoil?

If my state of being desires everlasting bliss,
then what causes things to go amiss?
Should I not have been able to see and tell,
when this game of love was not going well?

What once aroused all kinds of passion,
today draws contempt and only occasional compassion.
Is it my state of being that is the cause,
or is it the ambiguous 'just because'?

If love can make two beings into one,
how does each determine where the other has begun?
If similarities attracted us at the start,
now it's the differences that push us apart.

Moments that once were interactive and engaging
now seem irritating and often enraging.
What I once wanted to possess and protect,
today from that I want to disconnect.

From being consumed with sensation and pleasure,
the depth of which only I could measure,
I've reached a point where I just don't care,
embracing such loneliness, of which only I'm aware.

I wonder if all this comes from my state of being,
the dilemma between staying or quickly fleeing,
though not quite in the physical sense
but in my mind, thoughts and even essence.

And as I analyse my thoughts while they race,
I realise that in my heart, I still have the space
to forgive and forget the moments of pain,
and strive towards making my love whole again.

Love

Love is an emotion like the wind, that you can't qualify,
you don't decide with whom, how, when or even why.

Love is a feeling like a gentle caressing breeze.
You can't ever see it but you can feel it tease.

Love just happens often quite by chance,
catching you in its frenzy, and unending dance.

Love touches your senses, sends a shiver down your spine,
leaving you flushed and tingly, a feeling you can't define.

Love is tender and gentle in its soft embrace,
at times fierce and violent, a shame, a disgrace.

Love rules your world, even changes who you are,
struggle as you might from it you can't stray far.

Love makes you strong, as you clasp it tight,
making you invincible, when it's all going right.

Love reduces you to nothingness, as it gently fades away,
leaving you yearning for it, for even another day.

Love makes no distinction in colour, caste or creed,
it even exists amongst those who pay it little heed.

Love takes on forms, that can't be classified,
its height or depth, really can't be quantified.

Love touches all, rich and poor alike,
men, women both, get an equal strike.

Love is like, the 'beauty and the beast',
each one beholds, their personal feast.

Love lost can create, an unprecedented storm,
causing harm to those, who forget to perform.

Love can be piercing, like a needle-prick,
or festering, like an affliction chronic.

Love can make you see stars during the day,
as you lose yourself, in its gentle sway.

Love can fill your heart, with all its might,
help you soar, and your emotions take flight.

Love is like a weapon, that can be used to protect,
but be warned of the outcome, if you dare to neglect.

Love is truly, like two sides of a coin,
heads and tails, that you can't un-join.

So cherish your love in every which way,
for Life without love, is merely a cliché.

What is Love?

I'm not mushy
and certainly not romantic.
Too much display of affection
can even leave me frantic.
But I do indulge in an occasional cuddle,
and even a kiss or two.
And that's my way of showing
that I love you.

Poets wax eloquent,
about love and its display –
odes penned to sweethearts,
with lyrical wordplay.
But I am not one,
to get lost in this phase,
what matters to me,
are actions and not the phrase.

And my interpretation
of love clearly rises above,
the symbolic release
of a gentle white dove.
For it is the little gestures
that speak louder than words,
the obvious and unexpected
and even the absurd.

A dear one by my side,
as I sit and read a book,

cosy and comfortable
with the occasional caring look.
Holding my hand tenderly
up a steep flight of stairs,
are the little things that tell me
that someone truly cares.

A large caramel popcorn,
with hot coffee on the side,
while watching a movie together,
keep me gratified.
My favourite flowers,
turning up unasked,
on days of silent grief,
when my soul is unmasked.

We each have our own
personal definition of love.
Think of what's yours
as you mull over the above.
Is it words, lyrics and songs
that help you sail your boat?
Or just someone's thoughtfulness
that always keeps you afloat?

Companionship

What a paradox my Life is, I'm seriously thinking today.
Despite wanting companionship, I often push people away.
And while I enjoy my solitude, I complain at the end of the day
about all the exciting invites that just didn't come my way.

I read about events that I know I would so enjoy,
music, art and such-like, that could bring me much joy.
But then when I'm invited, I search for a ploy,
to refuse ever so politely, don't want to be a killjoy.

I find I no longer have the patience to meet and suffer
those whom I don't know well, the smart one and the duffer.
I seek no new friendships to add to my coffer.
Don't care who they are, or what it is they offer.

Maybe the voices in my head are the only companions I seek,
the only ones with whom any time I can honestly speak.
Is this a sign that tells me that I've let myself go weak,
giving up the fight to remain always and forever unique?

Or is this just an acceptance of Life that's changed me so much,
as I rely on family and friends who respond to my touch.
And the ones whom I cling to, who are my permanent crutch,
may they always hold me dearly and tightly in their clutch.

They Say, I Say

They say, 'The greatest thing you'll ever learn,
is just to love and be loved in return.'

I say, 'I've kept my end of the bargain,
but yours, I believe, is a cause for concern.'

My Imperfect Heart

I tried to join together
the pieces of my broken heart
but they refused to merge,
remaining still slightly apart.

Maybe the spaces left
were to store my unshed tears.
Yes I was left with many,
and unspoken words and fears.

They say love just happens,
you don't know when it strikes.
I say it also dies away,
leaving behind strong dislikes.

But can one really forget,
the moments in-between?
The ones that can only be felt,
the ones that can't be seen.

The times when you were happy,
the times when you were sad,
the intensity of the feeling,
the experiences that you had.

And what of my imperfect heart,
with pieces no longer in place,
waiting to be restructured,
longing for another embrace.

Should I try to fix it
or should I leave it be?
Maybe it'll fit perfectly,
with another just like me.

And since love just happens,
wait patiently I must,
and hope earnestly that,
my heart can again adjust.

Celebrations

An anniversary celebration
is really quite a sham.
A public display of affection
as if anyone gives a damn.

The love that a couple has
with time may rise or fall.
So why bother to declare it
when you best know it all.

I don't believe in celebrations
and pretending that all is right
when inwardly I'm itching
to have that pending fight.

So many actions determine
your mood on a single day.
So why this forced happiness
when you'd rather be away.

Sometimes we have a party
much against our wish and will.
To keep others cheerful and happy,
we just go along with the drill.

And what of the guests
who so sportingly attend,
many inwardly cursing
as outwardly they pretend.

So it's really almost funny
when you see it this way –
a party that you don't want to have,
and guests who don't want to stay.

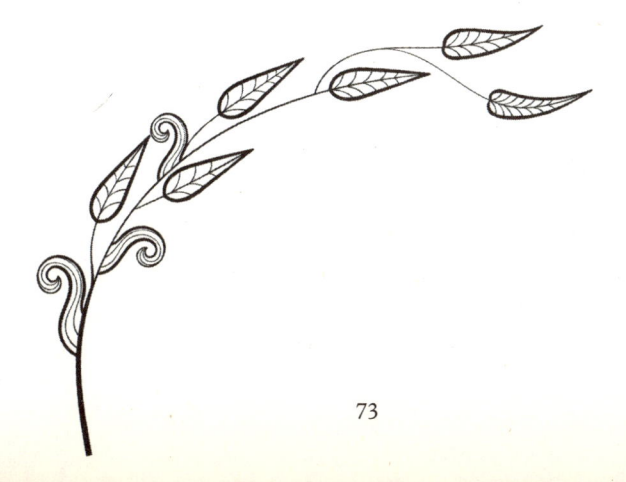

First Love

I believed he was mine and I was his,
so different, yet together sealed with a kiss.
Tears of joy and sometimes frustration too
held together by the powerful, 'I love you.'

I didn't plan or decide to fall in love.
It seemed ordained by the one above.
No romantic sparks flew, when we first met
but soon other women posed a threat.

How easy it was to get caught in the sway
of romantic gestures and words every day.
And despite the feeling that something wasn't right,
I just wasn't strong enough to put up a good fight.

The excitement and thrill of the touch forbidden,
constantly seeking places to be together yet hidden,
followed by the comfort, of being a twosome,
throwing caution to the wind, enjoying the outcome.

Accepting each other, overlooking each flaw,
hoping that the passion would never thaw,
revelling in the comfort of being in a cloud
of love and belonging, away from the crowd.

Eagerly waiting for the phone to ring,
whispering sweet nothings, a song to sing,
coupled with days of endless waiting,
where could he be – my mind debating.

Yet ignoring what others could see
that he just wasn't the right one for me,
not heeding when they told me I was wrong,
and that only to me he didn't really belong.

How foolish were the days of my first love
as I pushed others aside with a gentle shove.
More tears than laughter claimed each day
but I was so in love, I was scared to stray.

Till slowly but surely, the differences arose.
All that was poetic now turned to prose.
And as jealousy reared its ugly head,
I feared the repercussions and the words left unsaid.

But Life had its own way of making me strong.
I needn't have worried for I'd done no wrong.
And as I dried my tears and steadied my heart,
I waited for the one who'd from me never part.

Just Words

How easy it is to fall in love.
A few words can do the trick,
giving rise to an emotion,
so overwhelming, yet intrinsic.

So how do we ensure
that this feeling is here to stay,
when the path of love is known
to change every single day?

We hear the spoken word,
and listen to what we choose,
cushioning ourselves in happiness
of so many different hues.

But words without action
don't count for much.
So we wait in anticipation
for a gesture or even a touch.

Yet there are those who are smart,
and can play us like a tune,
leading us to believe,
that we're their eternal moon.

And when realisation strikes
that this was but a game,
there's a feeling of humiliation,
and maybe even shame.

Emotions can be intense,
as they blur our reality,
while we go from strong to weak,
as we seek alacrity.

And then there are times,
when just words are enough,
cutting through all layers,
even if we pretend to be tough.

The times when we believe
that everything is all right,
with the brightness of the day,
continuing well into the night.

Who decides why this happens,
or what is its cause?
Sometimes the only answer is,
an enigmatic 'just because'.

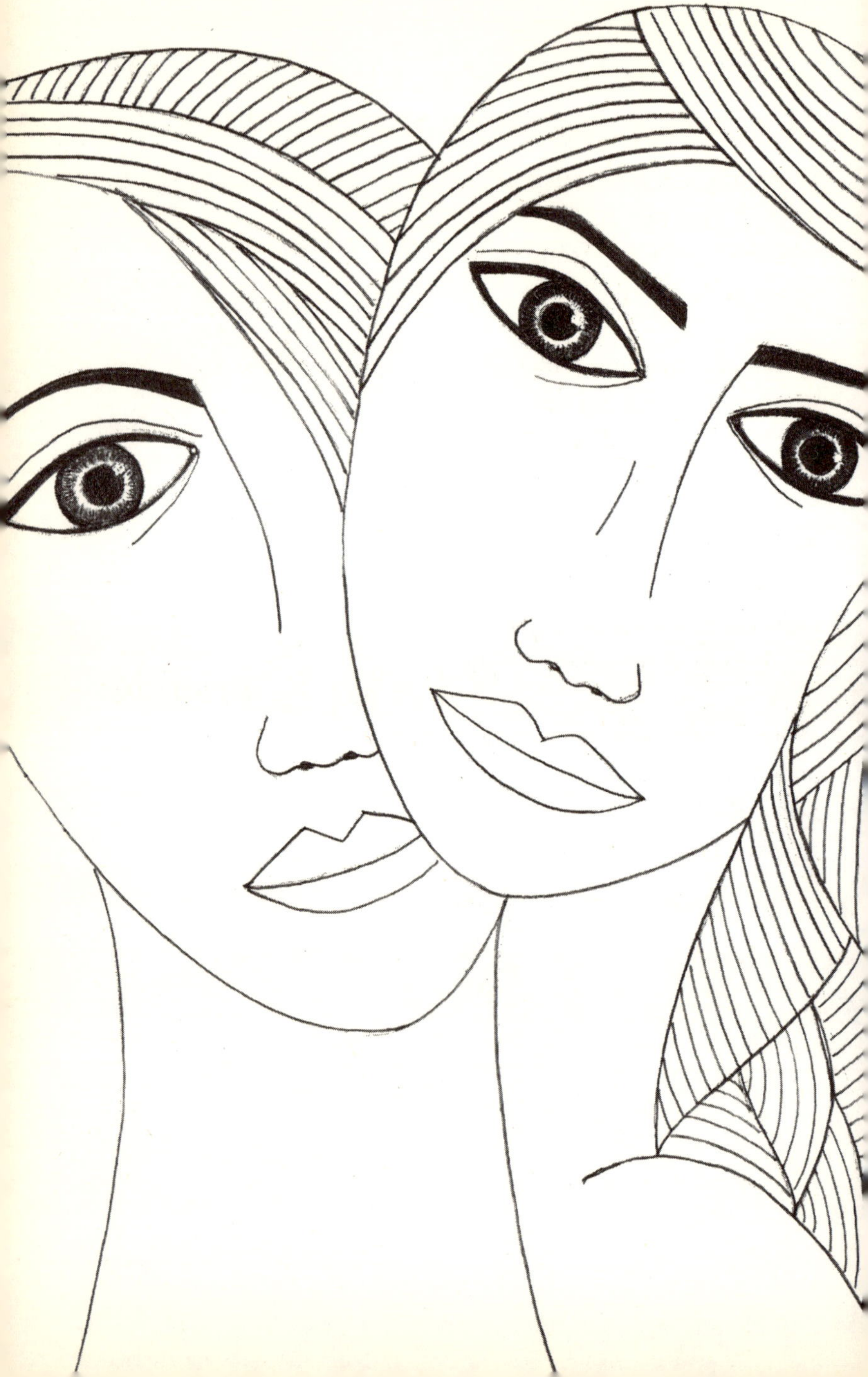

3

Family & Friends

Mother's Day

They say today is Mother's Day,
I say they are wrong in many a way.

A mother earns her stripes at the birth of her first-born,
and continues to hold that title till the day she is gone.

From the first day of motherhood, her Life isn't the same,
the changes that she goes through really have no name.

Care-giver, nurturer, friend and foe?
How her children see her, she'll never know.

She gives of herself without a second thought
that unconditional love can never be bought.

To a mother, her offspring are the best in the world.
So what if her vision is more than often blurred.

Social status doesn't dictate the emotions that she feels.
Unquestioningly she accepts the hand that God deals.

For a mother is the one who rides out every storm,
takes away your troubles, keeps you safe and warm.

She gives you her hand, as she helps you prep,
and only lets go, when you take your first step.

Through illnesses and joy, she's always by your side.
Your fluctuating emotions from her you cannot hide.

She's a master multi-tasker, and then some more.
For every little ailment, she always has a cure.

A mother can be fiercely protective of her brood,
all the while keeping pace with everyone's mood.

It really doesn't matter what age you have turned,
she'll continue to worry and be overly concerned.

She plays every role written in the book
but her own troubles, we often overlook.

And as her children grow, and need her less and less,
she really is the one they should continue to bless.

Though through the years, she earns your respect,
how often do you tell her she really is the best?

So to my dearest mother, I just humbly want to say,
'Thank you for everything and I love you each day.'

Saturday Night

The husband came home early to spend 'quality' time.
The kids were watching TV while sipping fresh lime.
I jumped up in anticipation as my husband I did sight.
After all it was the proverbial 'exciting' Saturday night.

As he flopped down upon the nearest chair,
I eagerly wondered what clothes to wear.
And then began an evening of so much 'fun',
Confirming why wives often think of a gun.

Husband and kids, each their orders did place,
as to and fro from the kitchen, I did madly race,
Serving each one, an individual meal.
Hey, is this a restaurant, what's the deal?

TV channels were changed to suit their common taste
while I pottered around, definitely a mistake.
Next, it was dessert that was a mutual demand,
Good wife and Mom followed the family command.

And through it all, I wondered aloud,
Is three company, and four a crowd?
Could just my additional presence, such a difference make?
In sheer frustration now, I was beginning to shake.

So, I slowly slunk out of my own room,
hoping on their fun to cast a pall of gloom.
Through common TV watching, bonded my kids and spouse.
For me, it was another Saturday night confined to the house.

I stomped through each room, doing this and that,
waiting for a commercial break with my family to chat.
Several 'breaks' later, my company was sought,
Aha, I was finally missed, I gleefully thought.

But no, it was only to clear the dirty dishes.
I'm waiting for a genie to grant me three wishes.
The wishes would be evil, of that there was no doubt,
don't think I'd be heard, even if I were to shout.

My anger was rising, I could take it no more.
So I barged into the room and slammed the door.
As you can guess, the evening ended with a fight,
and so did my dream of an 'exciting' Saturday night.

A Son's 17th Birthday

Seventeen is the age of a zillion dreams,
of parties and fun, and many extremes.

It's the age of being all grown-up and tall,
of confidence and aggression and knowing it all!

It's the age of struggling with exams and books,
of funky hairstyles and concern about your looks.

It's the age of believing that you're always right,
of sibling rivalry and many a fight.

It's the age of being, all hip and cool,
Of pants worn low, even to school!

It's the age of discovering just who you are ...
and wanting to sneak into that forbidden bar.

It's the age of dreaming about what the future will hold,
as you make your own decisions, some right, some bold.

It's the age of wanting the best gadgets to flaunt,
and of rebelling, against every parental want.

It's the age of gyms, workouts and nightlife,
while slowly waking up to the meaning of Life.

And as you study hard with numerous cups of caffeine,
we now know for sure ... you've turned 17.

On My Husband's Birthday

This special day, comes but once a year,
bringing excitement and loads of cheer.

It's a day, filled with fun and happiness too,
a smile on the face and good wishes for you.

On this day, you must celebrate the gift of Life,
with oodles of love, from the kids and wife.

Each time the phone rings, it adds to one's joy.
It's definitely a day, to just sit back and enjoy.

The fragrance of flowers, sent by friends so dear,
and thoughtful messages, from far and near.

A yummy cake baked, with so much love,
and heartfelt thanks, to the One above.

So these are my thoughts, for a husband so dear,
who never stops working, to enjoy the year.

Just switch off that laptop for once and call it a day,
and celebrate the happiness, of your birthday.

The Reunion

Two and a half decades and a little bit more,
a meeting of friends from every shore,
each with no inkling of what's in store,
but palpable excitement, as we walked through the door.

With warm hugs and yelps of joy we met,
a wee bit older but just the same yet,
we were still a college group, a perfect set,
though over the years into our lives, others we have let.

To Karuna dear, we owe a big one,
bringing us together, our hearts she won.
And to fun-loving Kalpita, a job well done,
as we sat together, sipping tea in the sun.

Sunil, the single, who now 'ventures' far,
Salil, also single, our evergreen sports star.
Vivian, whose gentleness, no years can mar,
with these special gents, we did once spar.

Vanita, looking different, caught us a bit off-guard,
how Renu remains so slim, we wondered hard.
Sweet Smita, with four kids, a surprise card,
wonderfully, our hearts the years have not scarred.

Medha, with her infectious laugh and memory so cool,
Jharna, a proud mom, who runs 'little palms' school,
Rashmi, so gentle, with the oldest kids in the pool,
and Punam, whose enthusiasm continues to rule.

This was the group that met in the evening so bright,
exchanging email ids and numbers with much delight.
Marvelling at our friendship and its wondrous might,
we happily faded into the warmth of the night.

Memories

Something to cherish
Something to behold.
So many decades of friendship.
So many memories unfold.

Who could have ever thought
this bond would last so long?
Days of lunch boxes and pigtails
in our memories remaining strong.

A knot once tied firmly,
can't easily be disjoint.
And even if the threads unravel
there's always that secure first point.

And as we weave together again
our lives string by string,
A new tapestry of experiences
to our friendship we each bring.

So spare a moment each day
to bring back a memory strong.
May friendship, love and caring,
be our anthem and our swansong.

A Son's 15th Birthday

Today is your birthday,
our dear darling son.
Fifteen years ago,
into our lives you did come.

It was a day of happiness,
a day to rejoice,
we were blessed with your presence,
your cry, a new voice.

Where have the years gone
we just don't know,
but our lives continue to be enriched,
as you blossom and grow.

Each year has brought with it,
pleasures and joys,
as you grew older
and gave up your toys.

The years have gone by
and now when we look up
we appreciate your many achievements,
as we watch you develop.

Our hearts also swell up
as we proudly say –
'That's our wonderful son
and it's his birthday today!'

A Son Turns 20

My dearest son, you've turned 20 today.
The teens now seem so far away.
We've seen you bloom and we've seen you grow.
Parents really can't ask for anything more.

What a fine young man, you've grown to become.
We're proud of you and all that you've done.
And as into adulthood, you continue to stride,
we'll watch your every move, with happiness and pride.

So here's wishing you a 20:20 vision
in every possible way
as you take on myriad challenges
in Life's pathway.
May good health, good friends and hard work,
your companions forever be
as you enjoy your Life
and the world's beauty!

Wrapped Around

There was a great party at a friend's place.
We had a blast as we invaded her space.

Her husband ensured that we had a lot to drink.
That numbed our senses, we could no longer think.

There were waiters around to serve us good food.
But it really was their attire that set the mood.

They wore kurtas above, and wraps below,
also called 'lungis' which perhaps, some of you know.

The trimmings of gold caught many an eye.
Wicked thoughts crept into minds, already on a high.

The hostess went into the kitchen many a time,
outside we conjectured, if she was committing a crime?

One friend swished her slinky sarong,
while her husband wondered what was going on.

A few others sat nursing their icy cold drinks,
while red wine drinkers were slowly turning pink.

We laughed, we joked, we ate, we spoke,
scandalising guests with words to provoke.

But the fun that we had, despite being bad,
made the party a success and for being invited, we were glad!

My Daughter and Her Tattoo

My daughter fulfilled a long-standing dream
of getting a tattoo when she turned sixteen.
This had been her desire for four years and more.
She had meanwhile checked out every tattoo store.

She profiled each artist and studied their style.
The design she had identified for quite a while.
A few family members had been kept in the loop,
but I wasn't even allowed to try and snoop.

Each week she'd threaten that the time had come
for this valiant deed to be finally done.
But I had no idea that today was the day,
when desire into action she would finally essay.

She claimed she was saying goodbye to a friend
when in reality for six hours her back she did bend.
It must have been painful, of that there's no doubt
but she sat through it all without a shout.

For as she does occasionally claim,
without some pain, there can be no gain.
So she bravely sat and endured it all,
as painstakingly, the tattoo artist continued to scrawl.

And when she came home, I had no clue,
during the day, what she had gone through.
So we chatted about things inconsequential,
nothing really important or even essential.

She then waited till her dad came home at night
and together, they both gave me quite a fright.
As she dramatically removed her jacket and revealed
that which till now she had so bravely concealed.

A tattoo on her upper back loomed large and dark.
In shades of grey and black was this amazing mark.
I was so shocked that she had finally done,
a task which in her head, she had long begun.

I was shaken and didn't know how to respond
for my child had created this everlasting bond.
It was my face that had been inked and done,
a copy of a photograph when I was 21.

At a loss for words, I felt so choked,
gasping for breath, I was really stoked.
Of a better tribute I couldn't have dreamt,
moved by what my daughter had dared attempt.

And each time now,
as she even passes by,
there's a lump in my throat
and I deeply sigh.
And hope that with this tattoo
twice the size of my palm,
my presence over her shoulder,
will always shield her from harm.

On Meeting an Old Friend

Ever feel that sense of excitement
that comes from meeting an old friend?
One with whom you've shared moments
that time just can't transcend.

A sharp intake of breath,
a quiver in your voice,
the sudden flashback of memories,
that leave you with no choice.

But to escape into the world,
of a wondrous past,
Reliving good times and memories,
that continue to last.

The good times seem better,
the bad seem less rotten,
transported into a place
of experiences long forgotten.

An easy acceptance of what
each one of us is now,
no overthinking the obvious
or the what, why and how.

Enveloped in the bubble
of the joy of the meet,
chuckling over moments
both bitter and sweet.

A sharing of thoughts
that continues to blend,
a fresh rush of feelings,
that seems never to end.

And so as I say goodbye,
with friendship back in place,
for new memories now,
I shall happily find some space.

School Friends' Reunion

I've read the mails and seen the pics,
of all our wonderful high school chicks.

I went through my mail, then went through it again,
each time, I felt a strange twinge of pain.

I don't know why they made me cry,
memories cherished and days gone by.

The glow of happiness on each face did show,
the sacred bond of the friendship you know.

We each have our sorrows that we wish to hide,
yet when we meet, we share our pride.

We each have our demons that we need to axe,
but when we are together, we just relax.

Oh, what beauty, in all the pics,
friends and loved ones, what a delightful mix.

And though the reunion has come and gone,
the fabulous memories will forever linger on.

And my final words, as I end this rhyme,
may our friendship always stand the test of time.

For a Daughter's 17th Birthday

Seventeen is the age of a zillion things
of hair and make-up and occasional flings.

Music and concerts and parties galore,
heartbreaks and angst and so much more.

It's an age of uncertainty and lots of pain,
of a little to lose and lots to gain.

Books and studies and so many tests,
so much to do and very little rest.

Smartphones and laptops are your companions steady,
and YouTube videos on how to get ready.

'Experiment with everything', is the name of the game,
defiance and confidence and a wee bit of shame.

Of thinking, you know more than the rest,
believing in yourself and doing your best.

The world is your oyster and you are its pearl,
a young lady now but always our 'little girl'.

Dreaming the dreams of a great Life ahead,
as you lie in bed with so many thoughts in your head.

And as you turn 17, we wish you the very best,
in you we put our trust and may God look after the rest.

So, our precious Daughter,
may you continue to bloom and grow,
as you step into another year,
and an exciting tomorrow!

Forever a Child

My heart loses a beat,
each time my parents call,
always worried about what
new problem did befall.

While I am blessed to have them
in my Life for so very long,
the fear of the inevitable
makes me worrisome and less strong.

Parents become parents
when their first child is born,
a title that is theirs to keep,
till the day they are gone.

My parents love me regardless
of whatever wrong I might do,
sometimes even blaming themselves
for what I've turned into.

In my younger days I fought
over every little thing,
not trusting one bit the wisdom
that age and experience bring.

I argued each time
the opportunity arose,
believing I knew better,
I continued to oppose.

Some days my sharp tongue
had a silencing effect,
a folly that I ought to have,
just had the will to correct.

But Life has its own ways
of getting back too,
making you reflect on the days,
when it was all about you.

And today after years of parenthood,
I have come to realise,
that children will never accept
that their parents can be wise.

And as I begin to say the things,
that my parents once said to me,
I'm just comforted by the thought
that they're still around for me.

Birthday Poem for a Father

Rarely has a daughter had
a father who's so smart,
whose passion and commitment,
come straight from the heart.

As the years go by,
and more closely we connect,
my awe intensifies in every way,
as does my respect.

The things you do for each one
with calmness and wisdom,
advising me through trying times
and even the occasional tantrum.

Your spirit is an inspiration
for me and all my friends,
guiding us through ups and downs,
and all the nasty bends.

And while over the years from you,
I've learnt about optimism and hope,
I continue to marvel at, on all matters,
your knowledge and how you cope.

Your level of energy and enthusiasm,
even at this stage,
often puts to shame others,
some less than half your age.

And as I wish you, in the years ahead,
a Life healthy and long,
you'll always be my perfect dad,
so dependable and so strong.

For a daughter, a father is a figure,
oh so divine.
You're one in a million, Dad
and I thank God that you are mine!

My Children

I tried to be a 'Tiger Mom', but couldn't get in the sway.
So I have these two children, who always have their way.
What I do think I taught them, is to do what is right,
and proudly I can proclaim, that they're even pretty bright.

Two kids raised in the same home, but as different as can be,
nature and nurture the same, an identical pedigree.
What then makes them dissimilar, in so many ways,
I believe I gave them similar punishment and praise.

What then are these factors, that mould our personality so,
the myriad influences, that determine how we grow?
Rage and rejection dominate the teenage years,
of confusion, angst and facing unknown fears.

Coming of age brings about changes so many,
a different disposition, and some adult agony.
New thresholds to cross, new boundaries to set,
becoming aware of what is your best asset.

Two different mindsets, two different souls,
encouraging each one, as they set their own goals,
hoping that my advice will help them along,
as they cross their hurdles and learn to be strong.

For as each individual acquires peculiar traits,
many remain average, a few stand amongst the greats.
But as a mom I can only hope to do my best,
provide a conducive environment till they remain in my nest.

Giving them what I trust are the lessons of Life,
believing in yourself and gently handling strife,
for the road to success is long and hard,
so choose your battles wisely to remain unscarred.

And as my children set out, each on their personal quest,
I sincerely hope they'll work hard and ace every test,
for as we all know that though Life's not fair,
just have faith in yourself and never ever despair.

On Friendship

When a dear friend leaves, cry if you must.
Wash away the cobwebs, clear out the dust.
The feelings that surface come straight from the heart,
of good times together and those spent apart.

And with each goodbye comes sadness and fear,
of days away from someone, who is so dear.
And this is truly what good friends are about,
bringing cheer, then sadness, as they flit in and out.

Yet with every tear shed and that one last hug,
comes an emptiness that can't be cured by any drug.
Then faith and hope our new friends do become.
As we wait for another dear one to come.

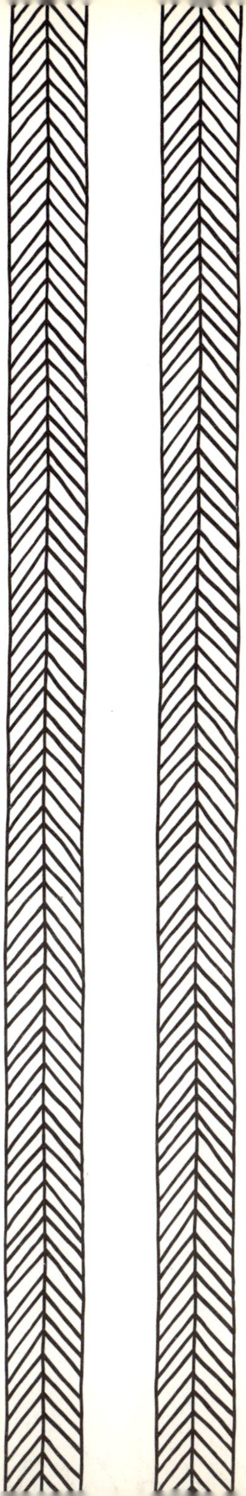

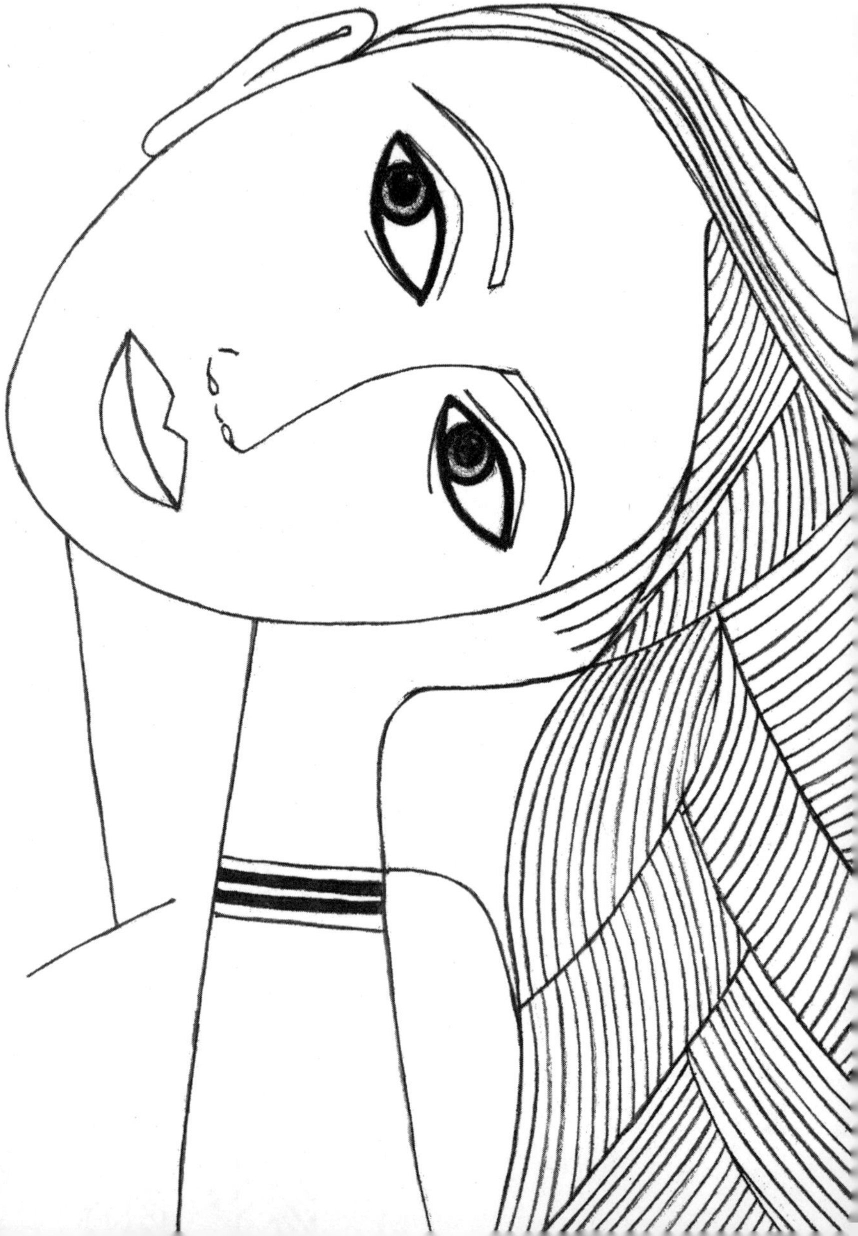

4

Fears & Frustrations

Demons

They are all around me,
yet I feel alone.
Is this fear of loneliness,
or just demons in my soul?

Why or how has this happened?
I have no answer yet.
But I continue to feel anxious,
as in my mind they are set.

I struggle with each day,
since push them away I must.
But they continue to torment me,
as upon me they are thrust.

Who or what are they,
I really do not know.
But in my mind and body,
they just seem to grow.

I will be strong, I shout,
to frighten them away.
But they just laugh at me,
and continue to stay.

But wait, I'm almost sure,
I counted one less today.
Something's worked, I'll just keep trying,
and send them all away.

The Future?

My Life is full of stress, it showed up in a card,
I had a Tarot reading done and now it's hitting me hard.

Foolishly, we want to know what the future for us does hold,
and then we anxiously wait for each new day to unfold.

Must we agonise over tomorrow,
as we hope things will go our way,
often looking over our shoulder,
as we warily tread each day.

The Devil showed up in my cards,
smiling wickedly at me,
I looked away, then looked back,
from his gaze I couldn't flee.

I really don't know what to do, 'Stop partying,' said the cards.
The Tarot reader clucked aloud, as I saw my Life in shards.

I felt so bare that I'd let a stranger see
what in my Life lay ahead.
Fortunately, the prediction lasts for only two weeks,
is what she also said.

Hurray, hurray, so glad was I,
that new cards could soon be read,
so happily I shut out the Devils' gaze,
as the future I no longer dread.

Snakes in the Grass

My dreams are regularly shattered by 'snakes in the grass',
bonding with all mankind, no differences in class.
I keep hoping for transparency, like a clear-looking glass.
Alas, what I often encounter is vile and crass.

Each time my day with happiness I do start,
I meet a friend, who's interesting, charming and so smart.
The moments we spend together, they gladden my little heart
till I return home to find, in my back, yet another dart.

I like to believe in the beauty of all creatures great and small.
But Mankind, the most evolved, is the nastiest one of all.
And when the phone rings loudly, I politely take each call,
unaware of the fact that I'm being recorded through it all.

Each word I say, some nice, some inadvertently in anger said,
are thrown back at me casually and they spin in my head.
And yes, it's these very friends, who make me now see red,
as I reflect back on the times, by them I've been misled.

It's not too late I think, two can play this game.
Beside my trusting self, I've no one else to blame.
And when the doubting Thomas in me loudly calls my name,
I know that while I may not change, I'll just never be the same.

Conversations in My Head

Ever so often I have conversations in my head,
saying all that in reality always remains unsaid.

The face that I put on, the kind words that I say,
are often just a farce that I go through each day.

My deep dark emotions often plague me in a dream,
Yet, when I voice my thoughts, it's a long, silent scream.

I wait with bated breath, for the moment to be right,
yet, lose that very courage when the person's in sight.

It's not that I think unkind thoughts,
or have nasty things to say,
I'm just consumed by the fear,
of putting my reality on display.

How can I share my hopes, my feelings and desires?
What if I boldly bare my soul and the encounter misfires?

Will I have lost a friend,
who now understands me less and less?
Or will I have opened up a door,
for now her own feelings to express?

And as I keep talking to myself, aloud and in my head,
I wonder, if it isn't actually my own thoughts that I've misread.

Beware!

Google, Twitter and Facebook,
are slimy devils for sure.
After capturing our souls,
they keep hankering for more.

First they befriend us, then take over our lives,
know what we desire, on what each one thrives.

And soon we get caught,
in their all-knowing net,
as we search for and share info,
with people we haven't met.

Then gently we get lured into groups unsure,
searching and re-tweeting, even liking the obscure.

We're happy to be befriended,
and as the number of 'likes' grow,
we forget we might be interacting,
with the disturbed or a weirdo!

Just a comment here, in characters few,
compliments or criticism, that depends on you.

And soon, we're lost,
in a vast cyber world,
forgetting those around us,
as on our couch, we lie curled.

And the only exercise we get is jumping from link to link.
in wanting to absorb it all, we even forget to blink.

And so our eyes grow weak,
as do our bellies grow large,
while many important duties,
we just forget to discharge.

Soon we've cut ourselves away from the mundane bits of Life,
forsaking human interaction and even our nightlife.

Around work and responsibilities,
we keep trying to sneak,
that one last look,
as into our phones we peek.

The give-away beeps and special-alert tones,
demand our attention, as everyone knows.

So do we then complain,
as we embrace this new world?
I, for one, am happy,
to be a cyber nerd!

How Will it End?

The weekend has been nasty,
no peace or time to rest.
Just anger and frustration,
despite trying to do my best.
Accusations are being hurled,
verbal and written alike,
I'm in a state of anxiety,
awaiting the next strike.

My calm has been lambasted,
by phone calls galore,
discussing useless matters,
which normally I would ignore.
My husband and kids too,
are now inadvertently part of the plot.
As the issues burn and sizzle,
it's getting a bit too hot!

Who knew that my good intentions,
would result in passions so severe?
I'm surprised as I see,
the dark side of people I did revere.
The idle mind truly is,
the Devil's dearest friend,
as like-minded evil souls,
their energies continue to blend.

I'm fast realising that double-speak
is not an uncommon trait.

Hopefully these people will,
before long seal their own fate.
So, as I rise again, to fight off
this unnecessary outpour,
Truth and fairness will always triumph,
of that I am sure!

Exams!

The exams stretched on, I just couldn't wait
for the last one to get over as I planned my date.
Locked up in my room with a pile of books
with my focus, honestly, more on my looks.

Had my hair grown in the past few weeks?
Were those new pimples defacing my cheeks?
I knew that I had to look my best
and to boldly stand out amongst the rest.

But these stupid exams had come in the way
ruining the excitement, building up every day.
This was the age for always being in a rush
romanticising and dreaming about my new crush.

Who cared about English, Geography and the rest
when Math and Physics, with my head had messed?
Don't teachers realise what students go through?
It's like they were never young, but suddenly grew.

Annoying parents, constantly knocking on the door
wondering if I was studying, they had to be sure.
They too seem to have forgotten their days of fun.
Now they rally together and behave as one.

I heard the phone ringing, I hope it's for me.
I'm not the one calling as you can see.
But the silly instrument is out in the hall.
My conversation can be heard by one and all.

But at least it's a distraction and a welcome one.
The equations are confusing even before I've begun.
But sadly that call just isn't for me.
So here I'm back, studying wretched History.

Being Vocal

I have a little corner in my home and in my head.
It's the one I retreat to, when things are left unsaid.
There are so many moments I go through each day,
where my inner voice just takes over and I go far away.

I keep thinking about what I could have said,
but the words remained unspoken as I lost the thread.
My emotions overcame my sense and sensibility.
And now as I think back, I'm more than just angry.

I'm sure of my beliefs and I know I have a voice.
Yet at the opportune moment did I make a foolish choice.
I let my silence do the talking and maybe that was wrong.
Why did I lose my nerve when I'm usually so strong?

Maybe I remained silent so as not to hurt,
the one who chattered on, continuing to assert.
I hope it was my wisdom that guided my action.
I'm not usually known to have no reaction.

But many times in Life, it's better to hold one's tongue.
Especially in the presence of those highly-strung.
And does it even matter when no real harm is being done,
if the person rambles on with gay abandon?

So in my little corner, as I sit and think things through,
I know that many others will share my point of view.
Who really doesn't like the sound of their own voice,
but being silent or vocal, really is your own choice?

It's War!

We glare at each other from two ends of the lawn.
Am I the reigning queen or just a mere pawn?
Should I step aside or move forward to attack?
Wish we could meet halfway and have a mutual pact.
Why must we go through this silly, futile act?
Watching and waiting for the other to move, to react.

We waste precious time on things and trivial arguments,
caught in the crossfire of unforeseen events.
Let's retire our egos and towards a common goal stride,
we each have a lot to lose, so let's put aside our pride.
Mistrust and suspicion, these devils go hand-in-hand,
before we even realise, we've taken an opposing stand.

How easy it is to allow a misunderstanding to grow,
developing into a mighty war from just a little row.
We waste our energies thinking many a nasty thought,
wondering how in this situation, unawares we've been caught.
Maybe I'm being naïve to believe this animosity can end,
with a calm head, firm hand-shake and a head willing to bend.

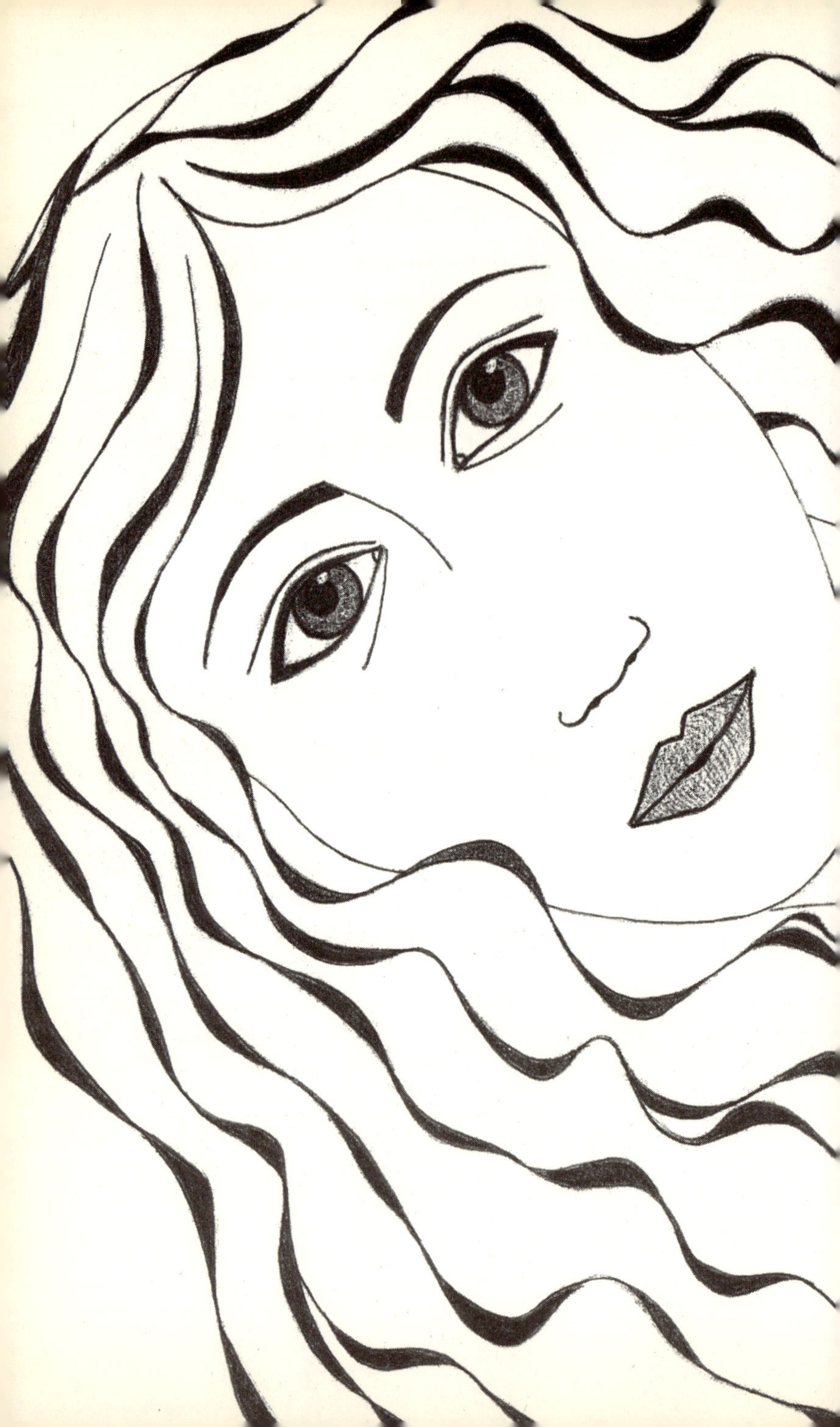

5

Happiness & Hope

Ode to an Educator

We were young, we were restless,
we wanted to explore.
Then along came this Teacher,
imposingly through the door.

She opened our minds to worlds
we didn't really know,
she threw us many challenges,
then dared us to seek out more.

From above-the-knee uniforms,
to dress-as-you-like day,
she led us, upheld us,
but never let us stray.

We learned Social Studies
and what ethnocentricity meant.
We learned to appreciate differences
on convictions not to relent.

Her booming voice over the mike,
though we ever so often heard,
we were taught to express ourselves,
often beyond the spoken word.

Theatre and elocution were ladders,
we oh-so easily climbed,
our school's festival of one-act plays,
were truly one-of-a-kind.

The 'exploration' sessions,
on Fridays after school,
taught us many a forbidden thing,
oh, we felt so cool.

This special Teacher into our lives,
brought much glee,
and we eighth graders
were suddenly high-spirited and free.

For as our developing minds
devoured books beyond our age,
our teachers explained nuances,
on every confusing page.

And today as we stand,
so confident and sure,
a lot is owed
to those learnings and experiences galore.

Through Man of La Mancha's
'Impossible Dream',
we soared ahead together,
a close-knit team.

Over projects and journal covers,
we slaved many a night,
yet cheerful in the morning,
all eager and bright.

Teachers grew into mentors,
some even became friends,
guiding us through the tricky,
growing teenage trends.

At inter-school events,
we stood proud and tall,
our school girls had that edge,
it was evident to all.

The years have passed, we've all grown,
our lives have changed so much,
yet somewhere through our meandering paths,
we still can feel her touch.

And as memories surface
and we choke back silent tears,
it really was this special 'Miss',
who helped allay our fears.

So rest in peace, dear Principal and Teacher –
an educator we'll never forget,
many have come and gone,
but you've stood out from the rest.

And as we continue to thank you,
from hearts you helped expand,
may God hold you forever,
in the palm of his ever-large hand.

The Obstacle Race

I bought some new clothes, then bought some more.
My wardrobe's full, I can't close the door.

So now the new lot in packets do lie,
I fear that my room resembles a pig-sty.

A walk through my room is like an obstacle race.
I have to watch where I'm going, lest I trip in this space.

The first round entails pushing shopping bags aside,
then a walk over the bed, to the other side.

And have I already mentioned my passion for shoes?
Every colour in the book should give you some clues.

Kitten heels, stilettos and wedges galore,
yes, the shoe-rack's full, there's no place for more.

And don't you dare think, this is just my greed,
I earnestly proclaim, it is but my need.

My girth has grown and I'm not too tall,
alas, most of my things have become a wee bit small.

So why hold on and not give up the rest?
You can't ask a hoarder to give up their best.

And if truth be told, I'm really hoping to regain,
my sexy, slim body and wear those clothes again.

Happy?

I guess I must be happy.
There's a smile on my face today,
thinking pleasant thoughts,
That just won't go away.

There are so many reasons,
to make me feel like this,
but I usually push them all aside,
lest negativity affect my bliss.

Is this feeling of happiness,
a reflection of my inner self,
or just mere rationalisation,
as I try to convince myself?

Is it just my thoughts,
that determine how I feel,
or maybe being pessimistic,
has just lost its appeal?

I'm rather surprised at myself,
for this reaction I rarely see.
Usually I wake up stressed,
and sometimes quite cranky.

I often avoid being happy,
for fear it will not last.
So even in joyous moments,
I tend to be downcast.

Maybe I had a happy dream,
so woke up in this state.
I really must find a way,
this pleasure to replicate.

I guess it could possibly be,
just 'mind over matter' today,
for I've decided to enjoy,
any feeling that comes my way!

Bonding

I walk into a room with slight hesitation,
unsure of reactions, a bit of anticipation,
meeting acquaintances, not yet quite friends,
wondering what message, my presence sends.

A greeting of warmth as my soul really tries,
to ensure that my smile spreads to my eyes.
Are people around actually glad to see me,
or do I detect an undercurrent of hostility?

Polite chit-chat becomes catch-up conversation,
but I continue to feel a sense of trepidation.

What makes us connect and forge a new bond,
as only to certain people, we instinctively respond?
What is that vibe that draws us close,
to people whom one otherwise hardly knows?

Is this connection a karmic one,
destined to deepen, though just begun?
Or will our paths just occasionally cross,
as we see only differences and no common ethos?

My attention shifts to others in the room,
thinking similar thoughts, do I dare assume.

Some seem happy and it really shows,
but what goes on within, one never knows.
I push aside all doubtful thoughts,
try to mingle with all the hotshots.

But I continue to wonder, to them how do I seem?
Is my intrusion welcome, do they hold me in high esteem?
Some acknowledge me, some try to ignore.
Should they befriend me? They're not too sure.

But then within that group, I definitely see,
a pair of eyes looking intently at me.

And as we start conversing, tentatively at first,
exchanging pleasantries, though nothing rehearsed,
I can definitely feel a strong connect
as from the rest of the group we gently disconnect.

And find a quiet spot amidst the banter and noise,
judging each other while maintaining our poise.
And then somehow there's an unspoken attraction,
like old friends, we have a similar reaction.

And I stop in amazement, as I excitedly think,
I've made a new friend, there's definitely a link.

And in that singular moment, I begin to relax,
happy to be away, from at least a few quacks.
For within this group, I've surely found a friend,
and the rest of the evening, I can happily spend.

Living in the Present

How can I learn to live, only for today,
while often yearning for that which was yesterday?
Maybe it is the future that I seek,
and thereby know my Life how to tweak.

I live in the hope of a better tomorrow.
It could be happy or one filled with sorrow.
But my mind can only hope for better and best,
that surely is every thinking being's quest.

Rarely do I enjoy the moment that I'm in,
always thinking ahead of other tasks to begin.
But isn't this then what Life really is all about?
Always uncertain, riddled with doubt?

While faith and hope can allay my fears,
raise my spirit and dry my tears,
I continue to let the little things affect me so,
like a maid's absence or a creaking door.

I often sit thinking thoughtless thoughts,
with butterflies in my stomach and gut in knots,
of the passage of time as it ebbs away,
of unfinished tasks and passions gone astray.

So how then can I enjoy what is the present,
sift through the clutter make it all coherent,
embrace the moment for what it's worth,
not overthink things and remain inert?

Every movement of the clock cuts down my Life,
a reality as sharp, as a brand new knife.
I really must learn to just stop and savour,
all that I have and become bold and braver.

Live for today and not needlessly dwell,
for what is to be, only time will tell.
And with each hour, embrace the here and now,
good or bad, make it matter somehow.

For only then can my soul rejoice,
drown out the annoying inside voice,
accept each day as it's meant to be,
push aside self-doubts and enjoy reality.

And maybe then, I'll appreciate the present,
learn to accept and omit the errant,
not linger over the 'what ifs' and 'if I had'
yes, for even just living, I should be glad!

What is Happiness?

If happiness is a choice then why do things sadden me so?
There's more to feeling happy than that which I know.

So where do I seek this knowledge,
that can gladden my every day?
I fear that only my thoughts,
can't always lead the way.

I'm told that happiness is free like the wind and the stars,
but the happiness that I know of comes with its share of scars.

I question its existence every hour that I'm awake.
Should I throw caution to the wind? What if that's a mistake?

I know I want to be happy but the moment that I feel so,
the fear of losing that feeling prevents me from letting it grow.

Like there is darkness after every new dawn,
I know that happiness and pleasure are all too soon gone.

So should I push away my happiness,
for its short-lived Life,
or enjoy the precious moments,
not worry about the impending strife?

Is this then my strength that I accept the changing tides?
Maybe it's the defeatist in me that often just overrides.

But if happiness is a choice then choose it well I must,
enjoy the feeling when it comes and share it with equal thrust!

My Friend's Garden

The flowers in my friend's garden, how splendidly they grow.
Their beauty, colour and grace are always on show.

The plants respond to her passion and concern,
a lesson for us all plant-lovers to learn.
The whites and the pinks, a subtle delight,
the reds and oranges, their colours so bright.

The wonderful fragrances invoke many a desire.
To be her student, I most certainly aspire.
The complicated names, only she knows them all,
as they bloom, winter, spring, summer and fall.

The flowers in my friend's garden, how elegantly they grow.
Their beauty, colour and grace are always on show.

Maybe it's the love, that on them she showers,
or the music she plays that makes the perfect flowers.
Oh how I wish that I had her green fingers,
to nurture such beauty and a fragrance that lingers.

And as I recreate her garden in my mind,
I know that towards nature, I shall always be inclined.
And with this thought, I must try and resurrect,
my little flower pots that I need to protect.

The flowers in my friend's garden, how magnificently they grow.
Their beauty, colour and grace are always on show.

On Happiness

We repeat the same old stories
to those who are so dear,
retelling our woes and troubles,
for responses we want to hear.

It's in the comfort of our friends,
whose replies we can predict,
that we lay bare our very soul
and expose where we've been hit.

I want to believe that I'm happy,
but how can I confidently know?
So I guess if I'm not unhappy,
then it really must be so.

And how do I measure,
what my happiness quotient is?
Is there some kind of a chart
or do I merely rely on my fizz?

Does my being effervescent,
mean that I'm happier today?
Then how do I interpret,
the bubbles that just float away?

And does my smile depict my joy,
or does it just appear,
to mask that I feel some guilt
and perhaps a little fear?

It's little things that raise my spirits,
through each and every day,
but sometimes it's the smallest things,
that can take my joy away.

A picture here, a sentence there,
an experience unexpected,
can take away that happy feeling
and leave me so dejected.

So if I know what unhappiness
is, then the opposite must also be true,
that happiness exists within each of us,
we just have to let it through.

The Sum Total

Today I've decided to put
my mathematical skills to test,
subtracting sadness from the total,
and adding happiness to the rest,
multiplying all my joys,
and dividing each sorrow too,
and hoping that the sum total,
will give me a better value.

Life is an equation
and balance it we must,
find the common denominator
and make it more robust,
raise the value if it's low,
and control a rise too high,
derive the perfect equation
and then let it multiply.

And as each experience,
I continue to add,
counting all my blessings,
for which I am glad
I mustn't forget to measure,
the percentage of my sorrows,
as I create the best quotient,
for many happier tomorrows.

When Should I Stop Dreaming?

Life is full of problems.
We accept them as our fate.
Some catch us totally unawares,
while to others we can relate.

As one set of problems lessens,
another lot takes its place,
ensuring that we're committed,
to being part of the human race.

The irony of Life continues,
at every passing stage,
presenting itself in different forms,
as we move from age to age.

Each new challenge that we face,
seems more difficult than the last,
as memories grow fainter,
of the provocations of the past.

They say we've reached middle age,
when our memories matter more
than the dreams that we've nurtured,
and always wanted to explore.

Have I then, I wonder,
reached this critical phase,
for while memories I do cherish,
my dreams I still want to chase.

Sweet 16

The world was mine, I owned the space,
desires and feelings in a constant race.

The belief that each day would just stretch on,
fun and excitement not ending till dawn.

Ah 16, that splendid sweet age,
the feeling of owning every stage.

Seemingly confident but internally insecure,
the excitement of not knowing, what's behind each door.

Hiding from parents, the rush and thrill,
of sexual attraction, against my will.

The innocence of believing, I knew it all,
misplaced bravado before every fall.

Unwanted acne and active pheromones,
heightened senses and raging hormones.

The comfort of friends, going through the same
endless conversations discussing 'his' name.

Lust beginning to raise its head,
romantic thoughts to take to bed.

Yes, the world was mine, I owned the space,
the memories still strong that I can never replace.

Soaring

If I let my mind rise and my thoughts soar,
will they take me to the moon and back?
Will I float above the soft white clouds?
Will I encounter an alien attack?

Maybe I'll sit on a butterfly's wing,
and flit from flower to flower,
light and bright, a perfect delight,
to be loved and admired from afar.
Or should I perch on a strong tree branch
and sway to the song of the wind,
as chirping birds flap gently by,
some wild, some disciplined?

As an adult, if I have childlike thoughts,
will people around me laugh?
Will they think that I'm on the brink,
and tell me, I've gone far enough?

Oh carefree days that did amaze,
I so desperately want you back.
I want to be strong with my troubles gone,
not always bemoaning what I lack.

Struggles and troubles, anxiety and angst
are constant companions as we grow.
So cherish your dreams, let out those screams,
for where they'll take you, you'll never know.

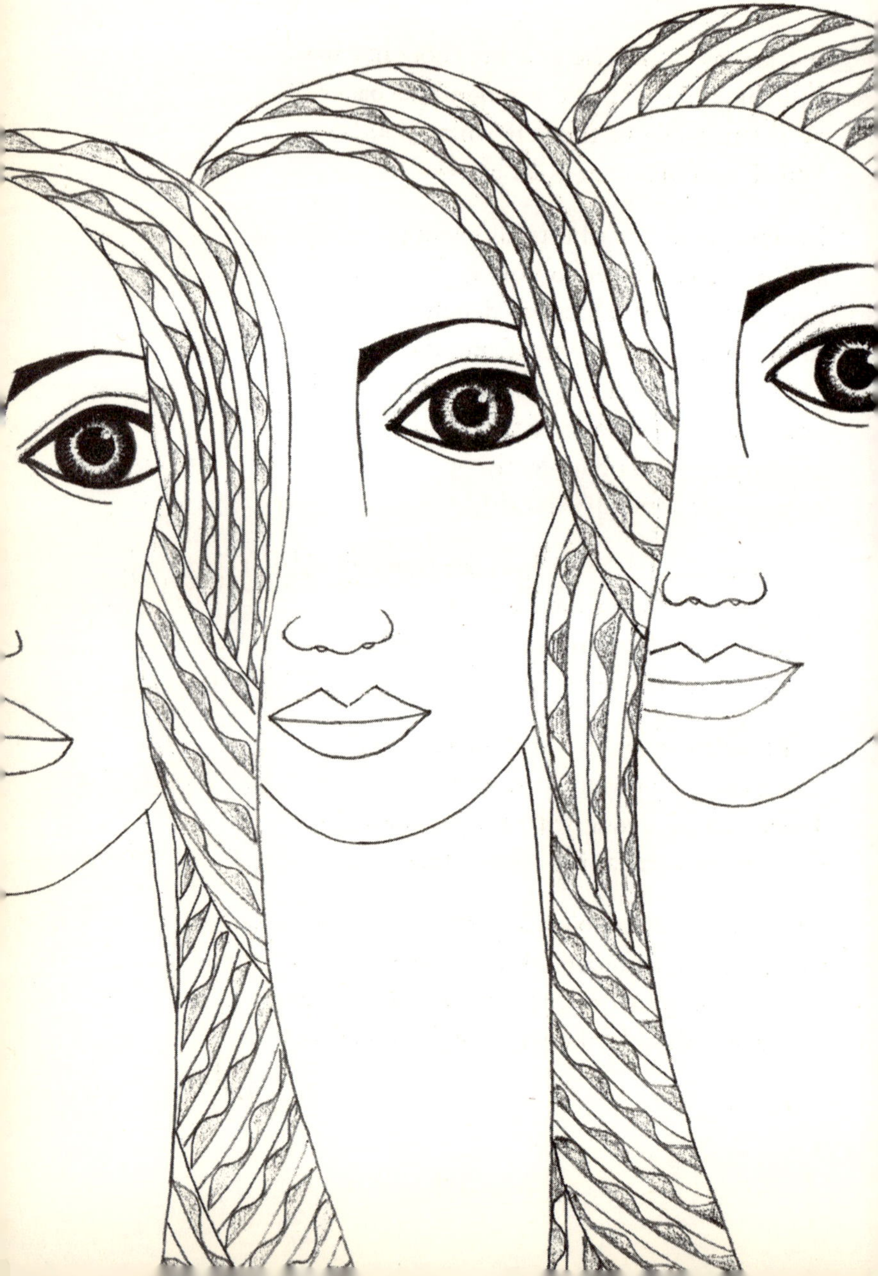

6

Despondency & Despair

Let's Rise

It happened one night when the city was going to bed,
a deadly horrific carnage that left so many dead.
The ugly head of terrorism had again reared its head.

It began so suddenly, caught us all off-guard,
the city was immobilised, it hit us real hard.
Hate-filled terrorists had used their wild card.

No shrieks of terror, just blasts filled each ear,
as unsuspecting guests, crouched numb with fear,
shocked beyond belief, with no time to shed a tear.

The city as usual was caught in a trap,
as evil-minded beings their 'job' continued to wrap,
our security forces and politicians roused from their nap.

Journalists and TV crew watched as if in a daze,
as terrorists meandered through a hotel corridor's maze,
leaving us all wondering if humanity would change its ways?

While grenades and guns took their deadly toll,
and innocent heads and bodies continued to roll,
our politicians responded, their eyes on the poll.

At home we continued to watch in horror.
Was this really happening or was it just an error?
As night turned to day and disbelief to terror.

Our valiant security forces succumbed to the gun,
brave yet reckless, forging ahead for a job to be done,
while the terrorists laughed at just another day of fun.

Our special trained forces rushed to do their job,
neutralising terrorists, were they just few or a mob?
Undeterred they continued, death their only reward.

Day turned to night as the hours ticked by.
Families losing hope had begun to cry,
as young and old helplessly continued to die.

While landmark buildings continued to burn,
our forces' dedication was a lesson to learn,
and for an end to this battle, did we all yearn.

Sixty bloodthirsty hours later, the siege did end,
with broken glass and bullet holes at every bend,
and many funerals for families and friends to attend.

The terrorists they say numbered only ten,
young boys in their 20s, some not yet even men.
Venom, bloodshed and hatred their only yen.

They came by boat to targets near the sea,
it was all about being on a killing spree.
The victims were but innocents like you and me.

The boys had ammunition tucked into rucksacks,
belittling political claims, of having broken the militants' backs.
Of voicing incorrect claims, the government had a knack.

And then the bubble burst, our apathy provoked,
anger and outrage, these fires were stoked,
capturing one terrorist alive our only gloat.

Thousands of people gathered to mourn the dead,
candlelit vigils, bowing in shame our head.
This time, citizens were roused to see red!

The politicians continued to pass the buck,
no one acknowledged, we are but a sitting duck,
the establishment had failed and we were now stuck.

When we point a finger at others, four point back at us,
whom do people vote for, whom do we trust?
Yes, we all need to act, that's a given, that's a must.

And now years later as the debate rages on,
kicking the dust and raising an international storm.
Unfortunately terrorism has no religion, no norm.

We blame our neighbours for instigating the attack,
while they feign ignorance – just a ploy or tact?
Whom do we blame and how do we react?

The city limped back as Life must go on.
Interrogating the captured terrorist as we sought his don,
while politicians believed to the manor they were born.

And yet the time has come for us to be bold,
our beloved country, we will not allow to be sold,
the future is ours, our children must be told.

As India is now on the global terrorist map,
our forces need sophisticated weaponry, to respond in a snap,
and a centralised command with no scope for any gaffe.

Yes, the time has come, we have to rise,
break class barriers, have no religious divide.
Seek out the terrorists that continue to hide.

We are a nation of numbers so great.
Now's the time to be united, no longer can we wait.
Solidarity we must show as our singular trait.

Let's answer awkward questions that we all ask.
What lies ahead is an onerous task.
Accountability must have a face, not just a mask.

As citizens of a democracy, we have a right to vote,
knock off corrupt officials, stop offering the note,
be powered by action and not just a quote.

And while we salute our heroes – quite a few,
sacrificing service staff and some strangers too,
the decisive turning point must come from you.

So, let us all join together to make a pact,
voting only for those leaders whom we know will act.
Bracing ourselves for how the superpowers will react.

And before we wake up to another unsure week,
within us let's look for answers that we all seek.
We are India – a nation that's strong not weak.

Let's try our best for a difference to make.
Do our little bit for each other's sake.
Make India a country, that will not quake!

Should I Worry?

A worrier I am, I cannot deny,
it's part of my DNA.
So how do I then train my mind,
to keep negative thoughts away?

I think I was born with the ability
of worrying for the world,
or maybe I acquired it bit by bit,
as problems at me were hurled.

They say positive thoughts
can change your mood, but I'm not too sure.
If that were the case, then a happy face
would surely make me secure.

Is it my idle mind
that dreams up disasters just waiting to occur?
Or maybe in reality what I crave,
is for more excitement to recur.

So many misfortunes cannot be controlled,
in my destiny they do exist.
But maybe if I think positive thoughts,
a few I might resist.

I sit and worry and sit and worry,
then sit and worry some more.
Wish I could throw those nagging feelings,
right out of the closest door.

I convince myself that if I worry enough,
for bad times I'll be prepared.
Unfortunately, when disaster strikes,
I continue to be scared.

So what can I do to change myself,
to give up this affliction,
between head and heart, stop the fight,
eliminate this on-going friction?

Good thoughts, good deeds,
a helping hand – a long way they can go.
So I'll give it a shot,
rewrite the plot and to the worries strike a blow.

For when troubles come,
I rarely am prepared with the right solution.
And all the worrying, only clogs my mind
and adds to the existing confusion.

So today I've decided to take my worries
and put them all to rest.
And when the next lot of troubles strikes,
maybe I'll just ace the test.

Delusion

I lie so often to myself,
that I've started believing it's true –
relationships and friendships,
even liking what I do.

Some days I don't feel so good.
So I just sit and pine,
imagining all the problems in the world,
are personal and only mine.

I wonder if a time will come,
when to accept myself I'll learn.
Give up all my high-flying dreams,
and to a simpler Life return.

I know I want to possess,
and protect all that is mine.
But then the unexpected strikes,
and throws me out of line.

I live a Life that seems exciting
when viewed from afar.
Don't want to expose what lies within,
so I never leave the door ajar.

Maybe the lies have helped me
accept my quiet desperation,
and face the glaring reality
of every shattered expectation.

Or are the lies just a shroud?
Maybe even merely a delusion,
turning all wrongs into rights.
Could this also be an illusion?

And even as each lie,
slowly morphs into a truth,
maybe I'm just regretting,
my long-forsaken youth.

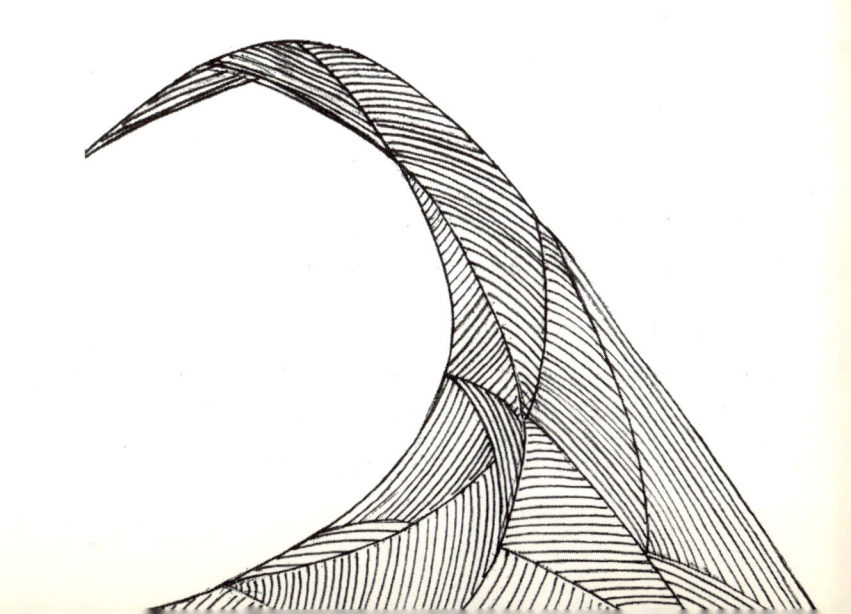

Chores

I don't like to cook and I don't like to clean,
or do any other chores that fall in between.
But if you ask me to read, write or sew,
I do it with a delight, that only I know.

And if there's no help around, I mope and cry.
But sweeping and swabbing I'm not willing to try.
And when the dust around begins to show,
and the cobwebs on the ceiling begin to grow,
I know the time has come to do my best,
to turn back my home, into a cosy nest.

And if a friend should drop by unexpected,
I scramble to hide what is old and not dusted.
For how can I let my image be tarnished
of running a ship, spotless and varnished?

I rely on help that is seasoned and trusted,
ignoring that which I know is not dusted.
But, despite treating them fine and paying them well,
their constant demands make my Life a living hell.
So I'm eagerly waiting for a gadget to be invented,
to do all my chores and leave me contented.

And if in my lifetime, this invention doesn't see light,
then I'll have to acquiesce and accept my plight.
That along with my desire to travel and rest,
a happy, healthy home, is an ongoing quest.

So alas, as I sigh and put down my book,
loading the machine and wondering what to cook,
despite my grumbling at the end of the day,
though exhausted I'll be, satisfied I'll lay,
till I realise that as the new day will dawn,
I'll still have to tackle that overgrown lawn.

The Clouds and the Carcass

Lost in the wilderness, not in body but in thought,
I'm blessed to be amidst nature and beauty that can't be bought.

Animals and birds of every hue, shape and size,
coexist in space, created for the young and wise.

Barks of trees look remarkably like creatures great and small,
taking on animal shapes and an occasional human form.

Yet amidst this serenity exists the circle of Life,
as predators hunt for prey in order to survive.

The carcasses strewn around, bleached white in the sun,
remain a gentle reminder of a weak one, by a strong one out-run.

With the soft white clouds above, slowly changing as they glide,
in the open jungle, a camouflage is the only way to hide.

And as I sit and observe in wondrous amazement,
the efficacy of nature's almost perfect arrangement.

I think to myself how different the human world would be,
if God had created us to live in as much simplicity.

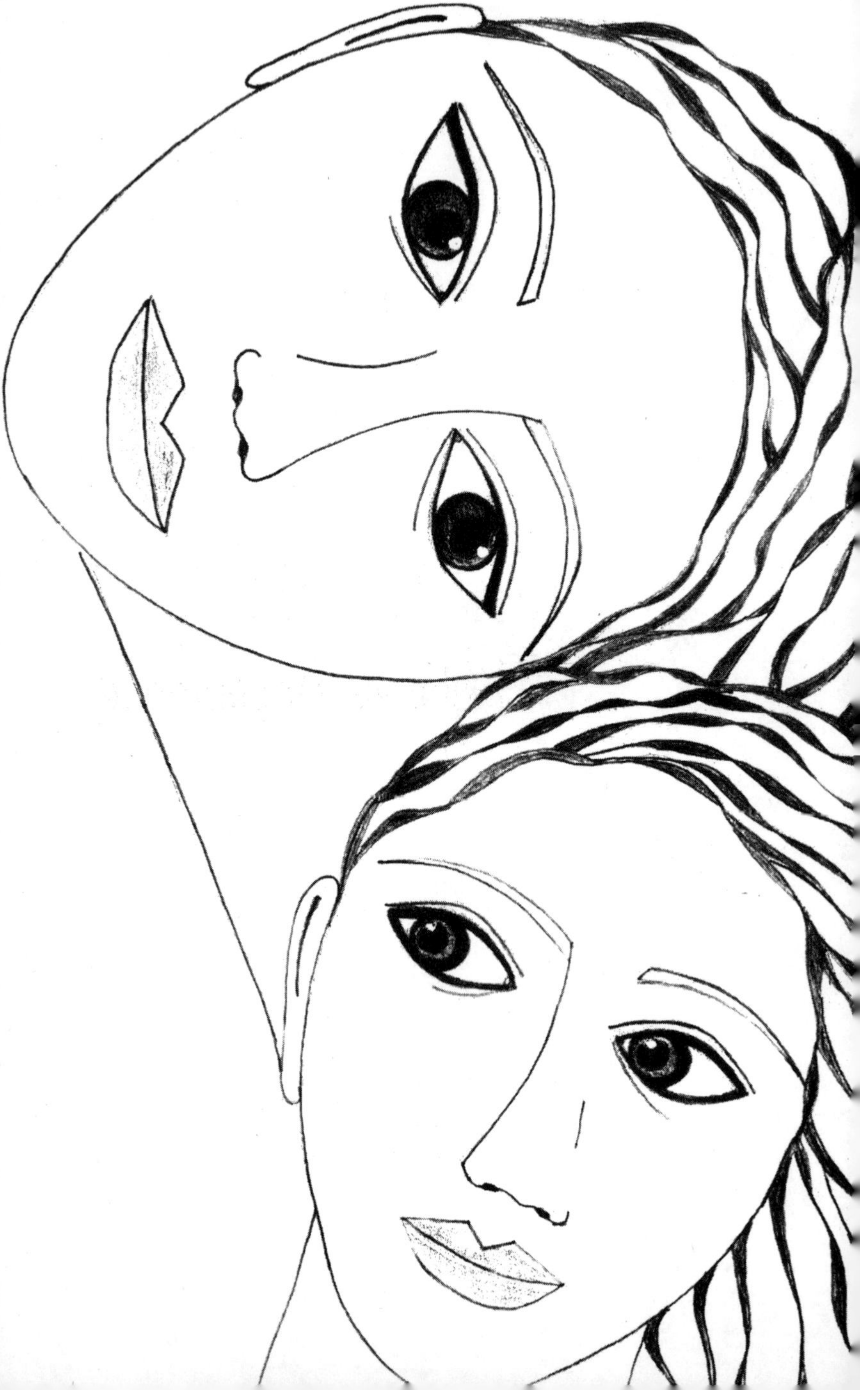

7

Ache & Acceptance

In Appreciation

Grumble, mumble, grumble,
and then grumble some more,
the help's again on leave.
Since morning, I'm answering the door.

The milkman, paperwalla and dhobi,
to name just a few,
each time I sit to drink my tea,
they arrive as if on cue!

The tasks I see ahead,
the list keeps growing longer.
I'm trying my best to take deep breaths,
to control my rising anger.

I'll make the beds, then tidy up,
next load the machine, I think.
Then milk to boil, fruit to cut,
and dirty dishes in the sink.

The daughter's up, baked beans and toast,
she wants for breakfast today.
I use every emotion to change her mind,
much to her and my dismay.

Dear husband has left home early,
it wasn't even dawn.
Meetings to attend, a flight to catch,
all in the early morn.

One breakfast less, I selfishly think,
as I sit down to cold chai,
plants to be watered, rooms to be swept,
clothes to be hung to dry.

So what if the house is a bit dirty,
it's only for a day.
I hope the help's back tomorrow,
I silently grumble away.

Bathrooms to be dried, showers to be wiped,
I like them spic and span.
These tasks are not for delicate hands,
I think I need a man.

Give me something to eat, shouts dear son,
as he awakes from his slumber,
I'm hanging clothes, I shout back,
that's definitely a pain in my lumbar.

The landline rings, I look around,
oh, where's the damn cordless?
I push some papers, they fall to the ground,
oh, no, now another mess.

And isn't that my mobile ringing,
somewhere in the room?
Don't they know, the help's not in,
I'm busy with the broom.

Ironed clothes into the cupboard,
and shoes into their racks must go.
Furniture to be dusted, bottles to be filled,
and I'm still answering the door.

I find the phone, chat with a friend,
my lament is understandably long.
I smile at the cook, praise her food,
she acquiesces to help along.

I guess in our domestic comfort,
we often do forget,
how hard they work to earn their keep,
while our demands are satisfactorily met.

Yet it's only in her absence,
my help I really praise.
I must remember all this, I think,
while negotiating her next raise.

And as I sit down to grab a bite,
my tired body to rest,
I think of how much we take for granted,
when we really are so blessed.

A Farewell to Breasts

I've had these twin assets for many a day,
initially firm, but now beginning to sway.
In my youth, to my beauty they did add,
for all the good years, I'm ever so glad.

For the man in my Life, they titillated him I'm sure,
for my wonderful kids, they provided nourishment and more.
But if truth be told, they've also given me grief,
no more tight straps to worry about – oh what a relief!

Each time my weight was on the rise,
I had to get new coverings, of a bigger size.
So here I am, ready to show them the door,
and get new ones that will trouble me no more.

And as to them I say my final goodbye,
I'll smile through it all – no hue and cry.
And with all my angel friends watching over me,
I'll bounce back in a jiffy, as a perky new me.

The Addiction

I woke up in the morning,
with just so many things to do,
but even before I knew it,
it was already quarter to two.

How did this happen,
where did the time go?
I know I haven't been that busy,
so how can it be so?

I glanced through the morning papers
and took a bite of toast.
My time management's good,
is usually my boast.

I looked at my laptop,
it beckoned me its way,
I know that I'm organised,
I have a well-planned day.

A little peek at Facebook,
WhatsApp and emails too,
yes, yes, I know I really have,
some important things to do.

A short call on Skype
and a scroll through some Tweets,
why do so many of them,
just seem like mindless repeats?

Oh, and there's a link,
that I can't help but read,
and a few more news articles,
to bring me up to speed.

Just five minutes more, I promise myself,
since it's almost time for lunch,
but then the comments grab my attention,
that's definitely a new bunch.

The doorbell rings, I raise my head,
irritated by the intrusion.
What's happening to me? I'm worried now,
I hope this is all an illusion.

I know I'm not an addict,
so how do I explain,
this fascination with the cyber world,
that is now my bane?

I've lost precious hours, I realise,
as the minutes continue to tick,
now through my chores, I'll have to rush,
I really must be quick.

The battery on my laptop,
is thankfully beginning to give,
and as I put it down to charge,
I grab a new chance to live.

The Old Nightie

I can't throw away my old nightie,
it's my most comfortable dress.
It envelopes me in its warmth,
just like a soft caress.
I think it was coloured pink,
when it started out its day.
But time and use have drained,
its vibrant colours away.

The tiny lace edging its hem,
no longer does exist.
But its comfort and soft feel,
continue to persist.
My family doesn't understand,
why throw it away I can't,
even though wearing it
makes me look like a frumpy aunt.

I darned a hole, scrubbed out a stain,
to give it a respectable look.
But like old burlap it continues to be,
despite the trouble I took.
I have so many more nighties,
each prettier than the next.
But I just can't convince myself,
to put this one to rest.

The husband scowls, the children smirk,
each time they see it worn.

I think they're conspiring with the maid,
to ensure that it's swiftly torn.
But how can I let go of something,
that swaddles memories in its weft,
I really want to cling onto it,
don't want to be left bereft.

Aha, I think I finally know,
how to make peace with my second skin.
I'll cut it up into a rag,
and continue the battle to win.
So though wear it I can't,
in its new avatar I can still hold it dear,
using it often to wipe the dust
and clean all that is near!

Chasing Unicorns

Oh Youth, I do miss thee.
Dare I think aloud,
where do I search for thee,
lost in some unknown crowd?

I'm all grown-up now,
and have moved on at Life's pace
so, are you still lurking around,
as an unfamiliar face?

Maybe, it's just the pieces,
of my broken heart that I seek,
the ones that remain fragile,
even as I speak.

The years have gone by,
in paces fast and slow.
I haven't fought any turbulent tide,
just moved on with the flow.

Maybe that's why, in my soul,
I feel a persistent pain,
of letting go the unicorn,
I was chasing in the rain.

And is that a broken piece,
that's piercing deep within,
of a passion buried deep,
or a new one trying to win?

Unrequited love, broken dreams,
regret for things not done,
maybe it's just a continuous search,
for the eternally elusive one.

And since my thoughts were always old
even in my youth,
Does that harking back in time,
make me seem uncouth?

So how and when do I decide,
to call off this ongoing search,
and climb down back to reality,
after getting off that lofty perch?

I say the time is right and now,
to let go of all such things,
Leave youth behind in the past,
and embrace what the present brings.

From Me to You ... and Back?

Why do you need my approval?
I sat and wondered aloud.
If everyone around loves you
Isn't that enough to make you proud?

Yet you prod me to say,
words that I don't really mean.
What then is this latent need
in my eyes so special to seem?

Why can't you understand,
that I have a different point of view?
I really can't sit back and condone,
each and everything you do.

I know that you are special.
I'm sure you hear that each day.
But that really doesn't change,
my thoughts and what I say.

I judge you based on how
you behave with only me.
Maybe a little different,
from that which others see.

And if I scratch the surface,
go beyond the obvious,
I'll be privy to the parts
to which others are oblivious.

And deny as you might,
the complexity of your being,
to me the joy is in finding,
that, which no one else is seeing.

Maybe one day you'll understand,
I have no desire to harm.
And truly feel contented,
when others acknowledge your charm.

And while our paths may cross
a few times and then some more,
we each need to sincerely appreciate,
our individuality, of that I'm sure.

For you are you and I am me,
and while we share a special bond,
I cannot be what I am not,
or predictably respond.

I do not know your Life,
or the trials that you have faced.
So can't even begin to judge your reactions
or the circumstances on which they are based.

So don't expect anything,
or even little or less,
but do remember that in my heart,
you're always loved and blessed.

Past, Present and Future

Is there really a past, present and future?
What is this concept of time that we continue to nurture?

Are we not reborn anew each day?
A person different from what we were yesterday?

If no day is the same based on circumstances around,
how can we then determine where we're actually bound?

And why does the thought of death scare us so,
when we know that we all have to ultimately go?

And isn't each day a death of the old you,
a reality that's understood by barely a few?

But if we don't live in finite time and space,
what is the point of running Life's race?

So we create concepts of ambitions and goals,
as we take on responsibilities and additional roles.

We convince ourselves that there's a reason for our feelings,
beyond the obvious and our apparent dealings.

A justification of our very existence,
a reason to continue with our daily persistence.

Our need for others and theirs for us,
relationships, family and all that fuss.

But is there really a purpose to this and to what end,
when we can't even determine what's round the bend?

Yet within each is this infinite potential,
coupled with a desire for ongoing attention.

So though we are a new person, with each new day,
there always will be a price that we'll have to pay.

For all our experiences come from the past,
with no surety of the future or how long it'll last.

Life, a Puzzle

Like the pieces of a puzzle
put together bit by bit,
I'm always searching for that perfect fit.

Maybe finished but obsolete,
almost whole, yet incomplete,
what do I add, what do I delete?

A little jagged, a little round,
what will bring about the turnaround?
Will the missing piece ever be found?

An unfinished corner, an empty space,
no clue at all, not even a trace,
of what to omit, or just replace.

Life itself is never complete.
New hurdles to overcome, new ones to greet,
each day a challenge, a fresh new feat.

Can there really be a perfect Life?
Eggshell smooth without any strife,
or cutting-edge sharp, like a new knife?

The puzzle, yes, one should pursue,
to almost finish, yet leave askew,
and finally end with experiences new.

And till I breathe, I must admit,
forever I'll search for that perfect fit.
And even as I complete Life's puzzle, bit by bit,
I know a part of me will always be a misfit.

Carpe Diem

What's holding me back, I do not know.
Why ain't I reacting, why am I going so slow?
In my head I know just what I need to do.
All that pent up energy needs an outlet too.
Yet each day I procrastinate, just a wee bit more,
instead of pushing myself, quickly out of the door.

I know I want to seize the moment before it's gone.
But the day goes by unproductive and then I am forlorn.
How did I let myself get into this sorry state?
It's only me I have to blame, maybe now it's too late.

Another year has gone by as I just sit and think,
Allowing inertia to set in letting things get out of sync.
A million ideas continue to enter and flood my head.
I really should hurry up and get out of my comfortable bed.
Greet the day as it dawns, streaming through my windowpane,
put my thoughts into action, there's really a lot to gain.

I need to do this for me and for myself alone.
And maybe also for my family and the loved ones at home.
Rebuild my self-esteem and bring forth my true worth,
use my latent talent and stop being so inert.

For Life is short and can change, as quickly as a wink,
leaving one scared and lonely, unable to even think.
Each day really is a fresh and new beginning,
and living too is a blessing, despite the inevitable ageing.
And as I think these thoughts, convince myself I must,
that there's still so much to do, before I return to dust.

A Dash

As I sit down and contemplate the complexities of Life,
the stereotypes, the paradoxes, the struggles, the strife.
The joys and happiness with tears galore,
what do I really want, why do I crave for more?

I am but a dash in the journey of Life,
a gap to be filled between birth and afterlife.
So must I make my memories vivid and bright,
or just let my imagination run and my dreams take flight?

There is no perfect Life, but some moments do define
things that make me happy, with which I must align.
Can I then embrace pleasure without any guilt,
believing in the convictions that for myself I have built?

What makes me want more when I can make do with less?
What fuels this greed within me is anybody's guess.
Why can't I just bask in the familiarity of my ways?
Why do I keep yearning for more adventurous days?

My head often plays games with me,
overriding what only the heart can see.
And as the heart sees, so does it feel,
while the head thinks, it's no big deal.

The inertia of being versus the busyness of doing,
the everlasting conflict of really not knowing.
Am I but here, for me and me alone,
or for deeds done, for which I must atone?

Who am I? I often don't know, my persona's changed so much.
I think, in the journey of Life, I've lost my spontaneous touch.
Should I then conform to exist in this finite space,
or just break free from all shackles, recreate my own place?

Time is but the passing of breaths, of movements fast and slow.
So why should I give it a value, why not just let it flow?
And as I continue to fill the gap with a dash big and strong,
blessed am I to have a Life and a world to belong.

Don't Forget to Care

My world can never be perfect,
that's something I need to accept,
ever filled with fears and doubts,
despite the ones I've side-stepped.

The many disappointments that I've faced
would leave me bitter you'd think.
But somehow the forces around me,
manage to keep me in cheerful sync.

Is it just my attitude
that keeps me in this state,
or mere acceptance of the situation,
and my belief in my predetermined fate?

If the brightness of the sun
can hide the darkness of the night,
maybe the power of my smile
can set somebody's day right.

I truly believe that happiness
grows when one does share,
just as sorrows seem less heavy
when unburdened on those who care.

So I consciously don't allow
little things to bother me much
and make a serious effort
with dear ones to keep in touch.

I also wish I could understand
those who don't bother to reply
to mails, messages or calls,
'No time', their perpetual alibi.

Maybe the day will come
when they too will get to see
the frustration of waiting for a response
that's probably not meant to be.

So as I resign myself to accepting
the differences that do persist,
I know that a perfect world for me
can unfortunately never exist.

The Open Book

My Life is like an open book,
each page has a story to tell.
Some are filled with excitement,
some with stories I'd like to dispel.

The ups and downs I've faced,
a few I didn't think I'd survive.
And the highs and lows of Life,
have taught me how to strive.

Sometimes the wait has been endless,
as I relied on my expectations.
At other times I've simply overcome,
my longings and my frustrations.

The future usually is uncertain
and even when I relive the past,
my memories seem so different
from the time when they were cast.

I rely on my experiences
to guide my future actions
but continue to be surprised
by the ever-changing reactions.

I believe I've lived a Life
that is good, chaste and pure,
but honestly quite unremarkable,
despite all I've had to endure.

And with a Life led so simply,
with no raising of the dust,
I've allowed myself to be moulded,
into the one who'll always adjust.

And as I turn the pages of my book,
my Life chronicled chapter-wise,
I wonder who would even care to read,
a book which has no surprise.

Nip And Tuck

What are nipples but pimples out of sight,
not having them will make you feel so light.

While the rest of us worry when they peak in the cold,
baring them in public is considered really bold.

More often than not they are just squashed in a cup,
your health is more important, than what you've given up.

So fret not my friend, for what you think you've lost,
your Life is far more precious to be nurtured at any cost!

And for that part of you that today is no more,
we'll smile as you progress, no need to feel sore.

And as we wait for you to recover with a leap and a bound,
seems you'll be the firm one, while we'll be jiggling around.

The New Normal

With 'happily ever after', giving way to 'reasonably content'?
The definition of normal is no longer what it meant.
Each day brings changes as new discoveries present,
thoughts and ideas so bold that they continue to torment.

Things as we knew them, now seem so obscure.
Even the so-called smart ones are somewhat unsure.
And what came with experience and was termed mature,
has been turned on its head by the new entrepreneur.

Each day as in this new world we struggle to fit in.
It's an uphill climb, don't know where to begin.
We look for silent moments, amidst the chaos and din.
It's a race against time that we usually don't win.

Even that which was once familiar now seems unknown,
as the seeds of discontent in our direction are blown.
Leaving us confused about what to condone,
as we cling to beliefs that were once the cornerstone.

Alas, time moves on and so with it we must.
Can't live in the past, only relying on familial trust.
Embrace the new as our mindset we adjust,
only then can we keep pace with the wise and august.

And in this circle of Life, we continue to exist,
for fear of anonymity or being totally dismissed,
steering ourselves to valiantly coexist,
as we accept the new normal as our destiny's tryst.

Cleaning My Room

I figure the day has come,
when clean my room I must,
since every step that I take,
raises a cloud of dust.
The piles of books upon the floor,
need a new place to rest,
and the clothes flung on my bed,
are certainly not my best.

The knick-knacks carelessly strewn around,
just add to the mess.
Old magazines and unpaid bills,
are now causing me some stress.
Shoes with broken heels,
for years have been crying for repair.
By now you might have realised,
that I'm just not going there.

The linen cupboard is stuffed with sheets
that have seen better days.
I really must discard them all,
say goodbye and then part ways.
The empty perfume bottles
that I've saved for their unique shape,
along with some old photo-frames
that are held together by tape.

Two bags containing more plastic bags
seem to be a silly joke,
as are the hangers of the suits
once considered bespoke.

The giant alarm clock that sits
on the table by my bed,
has stopped ticking a while ago
and now lies still and dead.

Oh and did I mention that drawers
that are so full of junk,
locks with keys long lost
and items in need of a dunk.
Old telephone diaries with numbers
of people I no longer know.
Long replaced by smartphones,
with photo-portraits to show.

The overflowing cupboards,
that I'm almost scared to address,
filled to the brim with clothes
of a size that once did impress
with bags and jewellery to match,
each outfit and attire,
alas, against my wishes,
there's really way too much to retire.

And as I lovingly touch,
each item that needs to go,
I have this sinking feeling,
which I'm sure you already know,
that today's not the day
when this cleaning is a must,
though perhaps with the blower,
I can at least clear some dust!

Momentum

Nothing is forever,
so take each day in your stride.
Move ahead with baby steps
do that, which you haven't tried.

There's something about momentum,
it creates a powerful force,
Steering you in the direction,
Of a very definite course.

Don't worry about where you are going.
just keep moving along.
Intelligence and intuition
will ensure you don't go wrong.

Life can change in a heartbeat,
so be bold and do your best.
Don't stop to overthink
while you're on this quest.

It's only when we move
that we bring about a change.
Sometimes it's only our mindset
that we just need to rearrange.

And then maybe a little later,
when you realise how far you've come,
you'll be amazed at the transformation,
and at what you've now become.

Often we need to be pushed,
that very first step to take.
Unshackle ourselves and move ahead,
staying back is the big mistake.

So bury your worries, throw out your fears,
don't think of the goal ahead.
The further you go, the more you'll know,
and a new path you would have tread.

The Memory Box

Ever have those memories
when you smile from ear to ear,
remembering events and moments,
that to you were so dear.
A happy thought here,
a cherished feeling there,
little bubbles of delight,
that arise from nowhere.

Memories are sacred moments,
that within each one hide,
and without much provocation
to the surface gently glide.
Your smile keeps getting bigger
as you relive the past,
thinking of those amazing times,
oh yes, they were a blast.

The opening day of college
and your first real crush,
the much-desired job offer,
everything in a rush.
The crazy music concerts
and your first big promotion,
all put together create,
such a happy emotion.

And it's these wonderful memories
that help tide us through

those times of grief and sadness
when you don't know what to do.
So fill your memory box
with happiness and delight,
and when you next open it,
it'll make you feel all right.

The Idealist

My boss called me in for what I hoped was praise,
thoughts dancing in my head as I anticipated a raise.
But what a shock it was to hear and suddenly find,
that I was in fact being pulled up, it was all so unkind.

As a young executive, I always put in my best,
working long and hard without break or rest.
But I was naïve enough not to detect,
it didn't matter what I could do but what I could project.

Drinks after work and back-slapping camaraderie
were the keys to my success as anybody could see.
But my idealistic mind just couldn't understand,
that what I ought to do was not what I had planned.

Days went by and my discontentment grew.
Each day brought more work and rewards few.
Should I sacrifice my ideals and join the crowd,
ensure my promotion, make everyone proud?

But no, I was made of sterner stuff than that.
I would stay true to my beliefs, not become a copycat.
I had morals that gave me a strong base,
that none could belittle or even try to erase.

For Life had taught me to be firm and strong,
hold on to my dignity, not succumb to belong.
For the true measure of one's success
is to hold one's own, when in a mess.

And so I trudged on with nary a doubt,
knowing the day would come when I could fearlessly shout.
I know who I am and I do what is right,
no peer pressure here, no unnecessary might.

And though admit I must, I didn't win every race,
often moving ahead at only a slow pace,
I remained true to myself and fought for each cause,
and when I bowed out, it was to a thunderous applause.

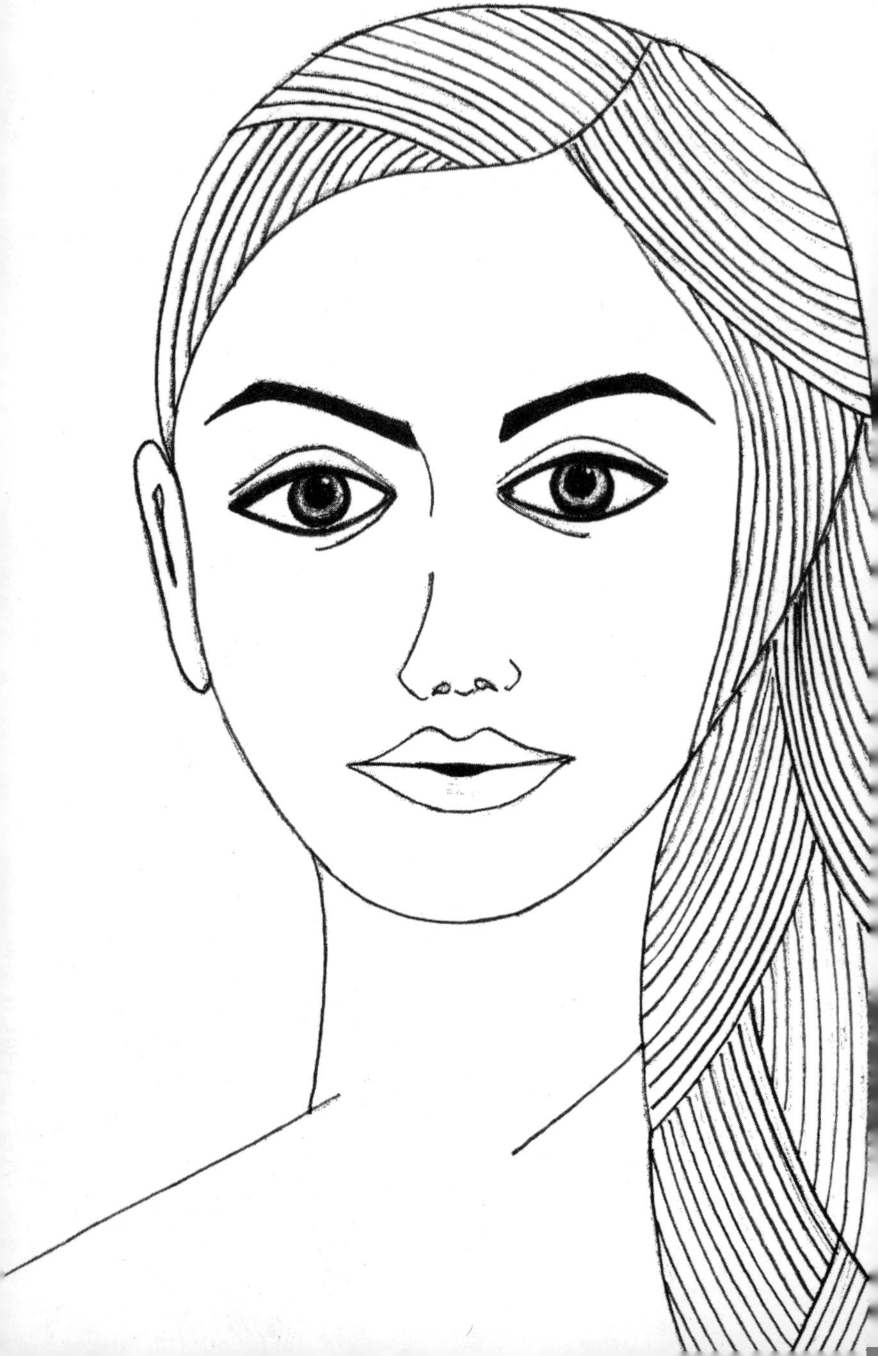

8

Questions & Queries

Still Thinking

There are days when I can hear
a ticking in my head,
is it excitement, fear,
or something to dread?
Maybe it's just the adrenalin rush
that my body is feeling
from the onslaught of tasks
with which I am dealing.

Sometimes I'm concerned that I have too much to do,
other times I have a different point of view.
That if I don't challenge myself then how can I grow,
for I have only one Life and no surety of tomorrow.

Some days I dive headlong
into things to be done,
other days I lazily seek
something more fun.
As I ponder and think
before I act,
reacting slowly
or without any impact.

So how does one get out of this bind?
Towards so much thinking, I'm not inclined.
Should I just do, then wonder if it's right,
Or overthink it, till I get better insight?

Will my spontaneity help
complete the deed well,

or will my analysis
actually help me foretell,
if what I'm doing is,
but the right way?
Maybe, I should wait
for just another day.

The ticking continues, it will not stop.
Maybe another blood pressure pill I need to pop.
That could be the reason for this anxiety,
or maybe it's just my sense of propriety.

And so, as I spend
another day of reflection,
feeding my need
for constant introspection,
the additional day I sought
is already here,
and over the same problem,
I'm still mulling, I fear!

Misfits

If I am imperfect in a perfect world,
does that then make me perfect
in an imperfect world?

If I don't conform to what is the norm,
then to which norm do I conform?

If I don't tread the trodden path,
will I lose my way in the aftermath?

If two wrongs don't make a right,
then the opposite of wrong
must only be half-right?

If there are shades of black
and shades of white,
doesn't that put shades of grey
in a different light?

If I must live in the present
and forget the past,
then why does history continue to last?

If there's no right time or place,
then how do I know if I'm on time
or in the right place?

If nothing lasts forever,
then there's no point in asking
the meaning of the word, 'everlasting'.

If the ocean's depth is never seen,
then what does, 'as deep as the ocean', really mean?

If something is deemed to be just perfect,
then why do I like my perfect, imperfect?

The Drama That is Life!

In the drama that is Life, I play my part.
What then is it that can set me apart?
Can I take the lead in matters of the heart?
Where do I begin? Just how do I start?

If it is my own path that I make,
carefully evaluating what is at stake,
then why do I still continue to ache
at every new, unforeseen heartbreak?

Do I live for myself or others around?
Can I soar as I please or am I duty-bound?
With my feet firmly planted on the ground,
will I ever be famous and world-renowned?

I go through so many daily transformations
of the mind and body, and other manifestations.
But are these just mere affectations
as I search for more challenging creations

'You only live once', is it just a cliché.
Like so many others, maybe it's hearsay.
So must I tread gently as I chart out my way,
or throw caution to the wind as I brave another day?

I rush headlong into many a race,
and return disappointed when I slacken my pace.
Yet to the world I show my best face,
can't afford to be weak or vanish without a trace.

And through it all I continue to search,
seeking impatiently as I advance my research.
Do I dare challenge or be left in the lurch,
toppling my reputation from its lofty perch?

Will I be known for the deeds that I have done,
overlooking tasks, that I did abandon?
And will there be a final race to be won,
as I burst ahead with stubborn ambition?

Maybe these are just games played out in my head,
keeping me from that, which I eternally dread.
A Life so ordinary that I've possibly misread,
that for glory and greatness, I have been bred!

Game of Chance

If Life is like a game of cards,
must I play the hand, I've being dealt?
Or can I shuffle it around
to make it more meaningful and heartfelt?

Should I play as a single opponent
or partner with a smarter one?
Maybe being a good team player
will ensure that the game is won.

Should I let others see
the cards that are in my hand,
or hold them close to my chest
as I evaluate where I stand?

If I discard an unwanted card,
will the new card that I pick
make the hand that I now hold
more useful and intrinsic?

And how can I determine
who has a stronger hand?
Will learning from the play of others
help me progress better than planned?

Maybe if I look at the cards
as just a game of chance,
will what happens next
be fate or circumstance?

And if a joker were to pop up
amongst the cards in my hand,
would it be a source of amusement
or something to quickly disband?

Just as questions, moves and counter-plays
in Life need to be precise,
if you treat it like a game of cards,
watch carefully as you roll the dice.

The Two Devils

I wonder who my bigger critic is,
is it the mirror or my mind?
They both seem to compete
as my flaws they continuously find.

Each time my ego gets a boost
and my confidence gets a rise,
mind or mirror is always there,
the truth for me to apprise.

And then the doubts begin
as I unnecessarily overthink,
looking for a vested interest
and revisiting every link.

The two Devils around me –
the mirror and my mind
can both be so cruel
and dreadfully unkind.

And as I look beyond the obvious
pushing away my delusion,
I wonder if the mirror reflects
my internal mental confusion.

Or is the mirror just a piece of glass
silvered to reflect,
the apparent and the visible
with which I can connect?

But then aren't my thoughts determined
by what I can directly see?
So into the mirror I peer,
hard and ever so closely.

And if I shatter the mirror,
will I have more peace of mind?
Or just more mental trauma,
which now can't even be defined?

And as these thoughts continue
to play havoc with my mind,
my reflection in the mirror
is definitely one of a kind.

Distinct or Not?

How can I win the battle
that my mind and body play,
resulting in a crisis situation,
that I face every day?

Some days my mind holds my body hostage
and paralyses me.
On other days my body
ends up reacting so thoughtlessly.

If instinct comes from the heart
and intuition from the head,
which one is imbibed
and which one is inbred?

And if the heart lies within the body,
then the head too, is a part,
so how can I differentiate,
how do I tell them apart?

If the heart within my body
can make me pine and long,
what of the thoughtful feelings
that my mind too brings along?

Though my mind is housed in my head
and my body harbours my heart,
they appear to be indistinct
and seemingly counterpart.

So as I sit and think,
with my mind holding sway,
I guess every movement that I make,
is just my body at play.

But then again,
confusion rises to the fore,
for it's my mind that controls
my physical being for sure.

And as I find myself getting weary
with this battle raging on,
there really is no solution
that I can hope to chance upon.

And so to sleep as I close my eyes,
I think it's for the best
that my mind and body both take a break
and give me a bit of rest.

Thoughts

I sometimes wonder if all my thoughts
are really second-hand,
already experienced by another,
sometime beforehand.

No thought is really original
as it stems from some source,
embedding itself in my conscious,
as an unseen resource.

Sometimes these thoughts are triggered
by an action or a deed,
which lies embedded in my head
like a slowly growing seed.

And as the days go by
and this little seedling grows,
it manifests itself as a thought,
though how, no one knows.

But then it leaves me wondering
who had the very first thought,
where did it originally spring from
and how was it finally caught?

What was its influence?
From where did it arise?
Is there an answer to this?
I'm still trying to analyse.

And isn't it the same
with even the spoken word?
How was it identified
from the first time it was heard?

History gives us answers
to the origin of many things,
but each one must decide
to which thoughts they must give wings.

So as I sit and ponder
and my mind continues to wrest,
second-hand though my thoughts may be,
they shouldn't be second-best!

My Mind

Sometimes I wonder
if my mind can ever be still.
It seems to be in constant motion
of its own free will.

Even when I try to calm
the thoughts in my head,
they continue to race ahead,
some even before they're read.

They say prolonged meditation
can reign one's thoughts in.
But if I can't catch up with them,
how can I possibly win?

Each time I slow one thought down,
another one races ahead,
always a bit out of reach,
and often quite widespread.

I spend the maximum time
with myself each day.
So I really have no choice
but my thoughts to obey.

I know that only I can be
my own best friend.
So if my thoughts are positive,
there will be a happy end.

But what of those thoughts
that aren't always 'nice'?
Filling me with guilt and remorse,
as they continue to entice.

How can I protect myself
from negativity and its curse,
modify my thoughts
to make them less adverse?

I guess I'll have to become
the most positive person I know.
Enthusiastic and optimistic
and start letting it show.

For if my mind can't be made
to stop and take some rest,
at least I should be able to
change its course and conquest.

Time

How can I catch time when it's running away?
Sometimes I need it to stop for just another day.

If I stop my clock, will time stand still?
And can I then restart it at my will?

'Time and tide wait for no man,' they say,
a gentle reminder of mortality every day.

But if I could only make it wait,
rework my Life, change my fate.

Have more time for unfinished tasks,
attending to all that anyone asks.

Spend a little more time with the ones I love,
before they return to the maker above.

Will I then have less regrets,
accomplish more as the day resets?

Release myself from, 'I don't have time',
as I stop the inevitable chime.

Will a little more time make me more content
or will I still continue my unending lament?

Of things left unfinished for lack of time,
just a wee bit more when I'm in my prime.

Oh, if I could only test my thoughts,
return to relive those special slots.

Would I really be able to use it well?
Who can say? Only time will tell.

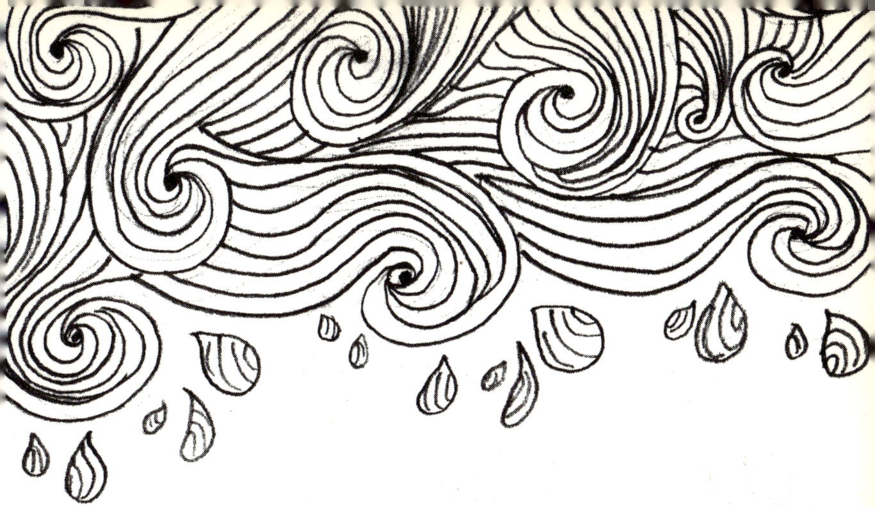

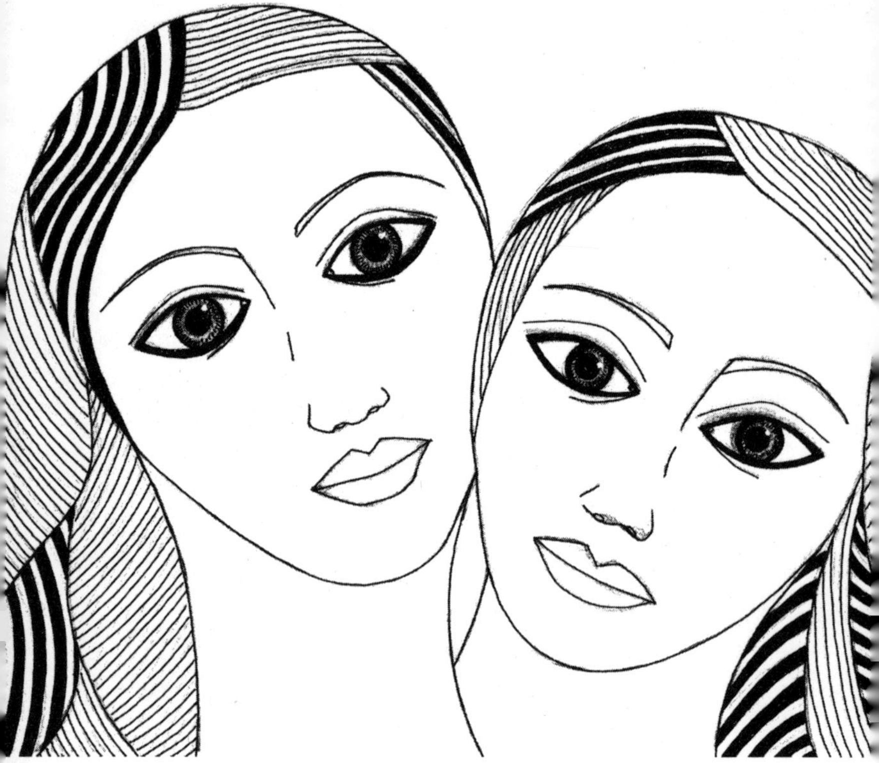

9

Benevolence & Belief

Simple Joys and Simpler Pleasures

How much beauty can a beholder hold?
How much happiness remains untold?

Three flowers in a vase give me such joy,
a painting on the wall for me to enjoy.

The multitude of green in the garden outside,
birds soaring gently as they swoop and glide.

Bright-coloured butterflies flitting from flower to flower,
in the simple things of Life, there's so much power.

Drops of rain glistening on blades of grass,
The smell of wet earth that nothing can surpass.

A sharp ray of sunshine slipping through a window crack,
the sheer beauty of Life never ceases to take me aback.

The baby-soft skin of a tiny tot,
the mesmerising appeal of a beauty spot.

The warmth of a hug from a little child,
the touch of a lover, electrifying, yet mild.

The taste of a cup of steaming coffee,
a hot molten brownie gives me such glee.

A call from a friend whose thought you just had,
oh, the richness of Life makes me ever so glad.

The marvel of a sculpture carved from a single piece,
the cosiness of cashmere and a coat made of fleece.

The excitement of a call that one was waiting for,
the rush of blood that sounds like a roar.

The intoxicating fragrance of a jasmine bloom.
A glass of chilled wine with a friend lifts my gloom.

The chill on my face of a crisp winter day,
so many things just take my breath away.

And, as I sit today with many a happy thought,
I thank you dear Lord for all that I've got.

Reality

The person in the mirror that I see
is that just my reflection, or is it the real me?

What is my reality, I pondered aloud,
do I really exist, or am I just a floating cloud?

To be seen, but not touched, yet admired from afar,
changing colour and shape, as is the need of the hour.

Am I a real being made of flesh, blood and bone,
since I can think and feel and even atone?

Then why do I doubt if I'm really here,
ever-searching, even filled with fear?

I know that I can love, lose and grieve,
but there's still a lot that I just can't perceive.

Who am I and just what makes me tick?
What arouses my passions, what makes me click?

On some days I can feel my existence,
at other times, there's definitely a distance.

So which is the me that I'm searching for?
I don't really know, I'm quite unsure.

Is it the physical me of which I am proud?
Or the emotional one who feels lost in a crowd?

Do my look and clothes define who I am?
Or are my thoughts and desires the real exam?

Maybe it's all me, pieced together bit by bit.
Not all is good, I must honestly admit.

Some days I matter, of that there's no doubt,
as I forge ahead in Life's roundabout.

But what then of those days, when I'm left forgotten,
feeling terribly insignificant and downright rotten?

Can I will myself to just float away,
only returning on a happier day?

And as I continue to question and explore,
what my reality is and then some more.

To the person in the mirror, I'll just say,
Reality or not, we're both here to stay.

Being Bold

I've decided to be fearless, I've read the writing on the wall.
I'm going to delve deep down within, my passions to recall.
How easy it has been to let myself slide,
and behind the cloak of excuses continue to hide.

I need to be inspired to bring forth my best.
So who will mentor me, whom can I request?
For if each drop, as they say, does an ocean make,
I must trudge on regardless, not let my resolve shake.

The world out there leans on those who inspire.
So my search is seriously on for someone I admire.
The list is long, of those, whose guidance I could seek.
This is my chance to be bold not meek.
Within each one of us lies a talent so unique,
it just needs to be exposed, given a tweak.

Yet, ever so often, I have been quick to judge,
harbouring stereotypes that refuse to budge,
letting the shallow and external cloud my mind,
like many others, I've sometimes been unkind.

And ignored those who didn't seem to fit,
falling short of expectations that I do admit.
But today as I desire to show off my best,
I realise that this could be every person's quest.

And as I grab this opportunity with both my hands
I shall look for the one who truly understands
that it's time and circumstances that do decide,

What comes forth, what stays hidden inside.
And as my mind and spirit, desire to unite,
I think I might have understood every introvert's plight.

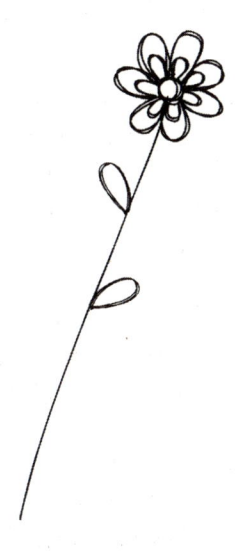

The Parallel Universe

For someone technologically challenged, like me,
the computer and the Internet is a fascinating study.
I just can't wrap my head around, how does it grasp,
what I'm searching for, as it holds me in its clasp,

And while I know it's programmed to respond to my kind,
I still innocently believe that someone's reading my mind
and giving me the answers to all that I don't know,
even unwanted information through links to follow.

I believe that I am strong and can resist at will,
setting boundaries for myself as I try to instil,
discipline in my day and time spent on the net.
Alas, my family views my obsession as a threat.

I like to learn something new every day,
a widening of my horizon, is what I portray.
But somehow, somewhere, I feel I'm lost in a maze,
mesmerised by ideas and videos that amaze.

Daily tasks are ignored and in fact almost forgotten,
as I slowly turn into a cyber-world glutton.
I pour over recipes of dishes I know I'll never make,
ignoring all dinner demands, my family's needs I forsake.

'Just one minute more,' I say with nonchalance,
as I continue to be fascinated by a new nuance,
reading and responding to what I feel I must,
resettling into my chair, as my body I adjust.

I start with searching for something that is a need,
Before long I'm caught in the clutches of my greed.
And as I keep absorbing information just like a sponge,
from the computer, my being, is difficult to expunge.

And so each day goes by, as I succumb to this exposure,
maintaining through it all, an outward stoic composure.
While internally I'm drowning in a deep, dark well,
living in a universe that is truly running parallel,

Reality and Life, and the here and now ...
I really must get out of this rut, somehow.
And as this thought in my mind rises and rages
the laptop battery runs out, closing down all my pages.

The 'Splinter'

I think I have a 'splinter'
that gives me no rest,
the one that prevents me
from often doing my best.
This splinter can manifest itself
as a nagging worry or doubt,
causing constant discomfort,
as in pain I sometimes shout.

The pain might not be physical
but exist it certainly does,
the unknown fear within,
the constant annoying buzz.
The one that I wish
I could just push away,
the one which also
is unfortunately here to stay.

I wonder if I could pull it out,
if only I knew where.
It lies hidden,
between feelings I just can't share.
I believe that this splinter
has lain undetected for years,
as I go through guilt and rejection,
and even confront my fears.

The problem with this nasty prick
is the timing of its emergence,

piercing deep within me
as it reconfirms its gnawing presence.
Sometimes lying so dormant,
that I even forget it's there,
then it pops up unexpectedly
to ensure that I'm aware.

That jealousy and anger
are its invisible barbs,
along with impatience and frustration,
the unwanted garbs.
And if I have to rid myself
of this permanent incessant pain,
I need to push negativity aside
and let positive thoughts regain.

Then maybe, this nasty splinter,
can be my saviour too,
for if I know what is the cause
then I know the solution due.
And if I can't pull it out,
I'll just make it disappear,
as I push it in so deep
that it can never reappear.

What's in a Name?

How joyous is the sound of one's own name,
an acknowledgement of who we are,
an identity that we each grow into,
and that a wrong spelling, can easily mar.

We become the person of that name,
and wear it proud and bold,
responding each time we hear it called,
reconfirming its incredible hold.

Our name is what sets us apart
and gives us that uniqueness too,
for as alike as others, we might be,
to our name, we remain true.

And though others may have a name,
exactly like the one you do,
annoying though it can sometimes be,
you know that they can never be you.

Ever wonder then, how this name,
was chosen to identify you?
Was it after much deliberation
or the best of a shortlisted few?

And what if you had been christened
with a different name?
Would it have changed who you are,
or influenced what you became?

And even if your name,
you don't always like,
how do you decide
on which new one to strike?

So more often than not
we each love our own name,
and it sounds even sweeter
if it gives us some acclaim.

Blind Faith

I tried bursting bubble wrap,
to put my mind at rest.
But soon it became a challenge,
as with my head it messed.
Some bubbles just wouldn't burst,
no matter how hard I tried.
And then I got so frustrated,
that I almost cried.

Who was the fool I wondered,
who suggested this insane game,
recommending it as meditation,
therapy by another name?
It really didn't serve its purpose
and actually got me riled,
and now I'm sitting sulking,
like an overgrown petulant child.

I hate these new-age gurus,
who pretend to be so wise.
I'm sure their own theories,
they themselves secretly despise.
For how can something so torturous,
become a meditative tool?
Maybe because there are many
who like me, they can fool.

And now that I'm convinced
that their words are but a game,
I'll continue in my endeavour

to challenge each one's claim.
I'll start by throwing away the bubble wrap
and the oft-used stress ball,
and the self-help books I own,
I'll start getting rid of them all.

How easily we put our faith in others,
even those we do not know,
treating their word as the gospel,
even if it's mumbo-jumbo.
Unfortunately, we doubt our intuition
and what dear ones say,
getting caught in the confusion,
of the information highway.

So do take help if you need it,
but do not shy away
from disbelieving what seems ludicrous,
or just not okay.
Find your own wisdom
from all that you hear and see.
And maybe you should also think
about easily believing even me!

Life Can be Extreme

Isn't it fun to live Life on the edge
between 'Should I' and 'I must', create a little wedge?
Climb on to a high terrace and lean out over the ledge
walk on a tightrope unassisted over a thorny hedge?

These are but metaphors of Life's daily thrills,
stepping out of one's comfort zone, just enjoying the chills.
The excitement of not knowing which desire your action fulfils,
but willing to risk it all, despite not having the skills!

Be your own being and chase that elusive dream.
One doesn't always need to be part of a perfect team.
Spead your wings, lift your spirits, go without a scheme,
for who knows what tomorrow brings,
yes, Life can be extreme!

The Decreasing 10

When you are 10 and a new baby is born,
the gap between seems extremely long.
When you are 20 and the other is 10,
to a different generation, they belong then.

When you are 30 and the other is 20,
the years seem to matter much less.
And at 40 and 30, you become good friends,
and to each other, even begin to confess.

50 brings forth a golden age,
to which even at 40, one can relate.
And as time goes by and bonding grows,
there's much similarity, a common fate.

Since 60 for me is still a bit far,
I know not, how I'll feel.
But what I know and of what I'm sure,
is the 50s will still appeal.

And as the difference of 10
grows less with each decade,
how we think and what we believe
are what need an instant upgrade.

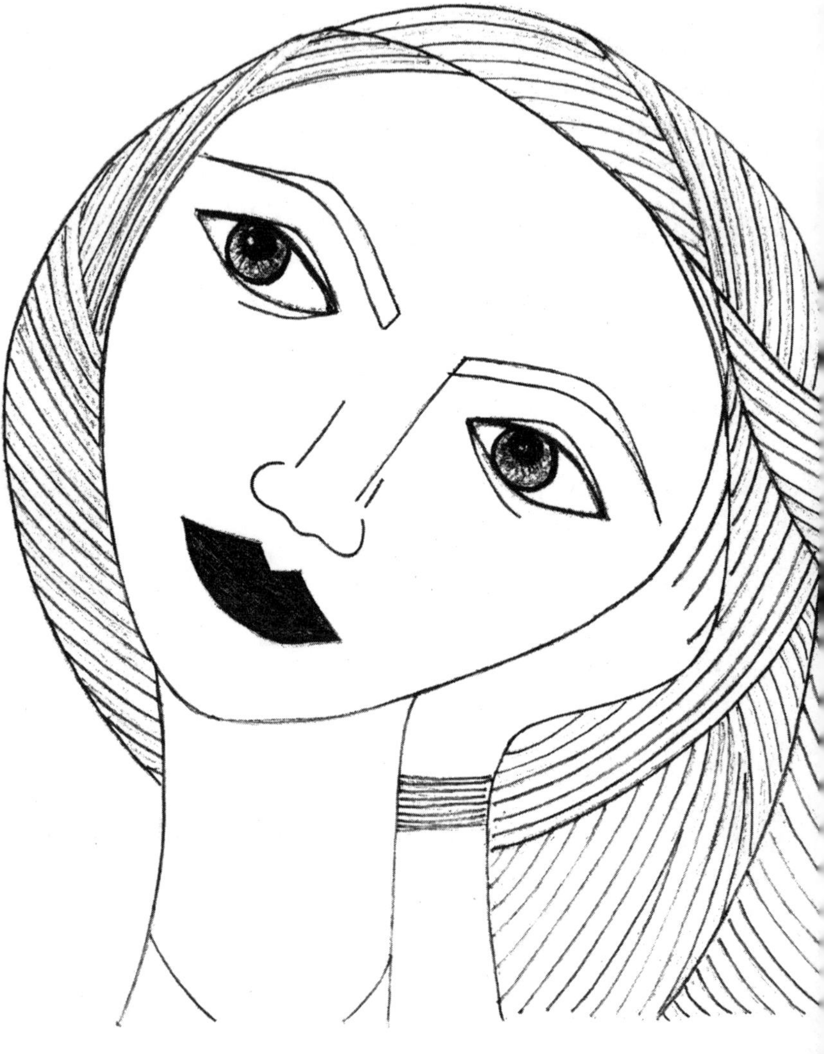

10

Dreams & Desires

The Illusion

I looked into the mirror and then looked away
had I really aged so much just since last May?
I knew that a spring chicken no longer was I,
had I to Youth said my final goodbye?

The kids are now older, their own lives they do lead.
I guess looking young is no longer a need.
And yet the fire within me does still glow.
Must I let it all hang out or need I go slow?

The voice within me speaks up at last,
'Chill,' it reminds me. 'Just go, have a blast.'
My mind is as wicked as at sweet 16,
with teenage thoughts, I strut like a queen.

So to my body, in a firm tone I do say,
'Get your act together, now do as I say.
Tuck in that belly, and that mouth do shut.
Eat what I tell you to, there's no "if" or "but".'

The time has come to turn back the clock,
bring back the 'look' on age, turn the lock.
Put on those shoes, go out for a run,
even if it kills you, pretend it's good fun.

I have but one body, so I must do my best
to look after it before I finally go to rest.
And with each pound lost, my confidence does rise,
having a healthy body would be my ultimate prize.

The wrinkles too relax, I think I'm looking younger,
a figment of my imagination, as I look closer, I wonder.
And did I just run that last mile?
As I smirk inwardly, outwardly, I smile.

Oh no, that's the doorbell, from my daydream I do snap,
breaking a sweet little fantasy as I awake from my nap.
But wait a sec, I'm sure, into a reality this can turn,
once you know you only have a few million calories to burn.

I need to worship my body and watch what I eat,
adding exercise to it, to achieve that perfect feat!
'Can I do it,' to myself I wonder aloud.
Everyone around will be ever so proud.

For my dear husband, a 'bomb' by his side,
for my two lovely kids, a mom no longer to hide.
So, I put on my glasses, all raring to go,
is that my grey hair again beginning to show?

Into the mirror I once again do peer,
the face looks back with a smile or a leer?
Oh well, think I, as I add to my list,
the overdue visit to the hair colourist.

Sometimes

Sometimes, I sits and thinks,
and sometimes, I just sits.

Sometimes, I eats to enjoys,
and sometimes, I just eats.

Sometimes, I talks to make others listen,
and sometimes, I just talks.

Sometimes, I reads to learn,
and sometimes, I just reads.

Sometimes, I loves in response,
and sometimes, I just loves.

Sometimes, I drinks for the buzz,
and sometimes, I just drinks.

Sometimes, I listens to hear,
and sometimes, I just listens.

Sometimes, I works hard for the money,
and sometimes, I just works.

Yes, sometimes, I lives for Life,
and sometimes, I just lives.

Expectations

The world is filled with people of every possible hue,
the ones who only promise and the ones who actually do.
What are the complexities that makes each one so strange,
wish I had a magic wand to bring about some change.

So, I often sit by the phone,
waiting patiently for it to ring,
believing in promises made,
that just don't mean a thing.
And as the clock slowly ticks
and minutes turn to hours,
my anticipation slowly ebbs
and expression totally sours.

I truly believe that reality embraces every shade of grey,
as our expectations swing from black to white every single day.
How easily we handover our happiness quotient to another,
parent, sibling, friend or foe and especially a lover.

We often can't curb our emotions,
they surface without control,
if only we could lead them to
a predetermined goal.
But then I guess that Life would lose
a little bit of charm,
if predictability became the norm
and we lost the power to disarm.

My Diamond

I dream of owning a diamond,
a sparkler with a brilliant cut,
set in prongs of molten gold,
from my finger it should jut.
For only then, will it be noticed,
for its clarity and its size,
leaving people guessing,
how I acquired this precious prize.
And the looks of envy
that I know will come my way,
as it draws attention,
will surely make my day.

Some might question its authenticity,
while others will question its worth,
I really don't care what they think,
what info they manage to unearth.
For this precious gem I know
will one day come my way,
after the long years of penance
and the modest gleanings of each day.

The only problem is, as my savings grow in size,
my desire for what I really want also amplifies.
And just when I thought, I finally have
enough to buy this rock,
I realise that I need those funds,
more essential things to restock.
And so I push aside my want,

my desire and my need,
convince myself it's just a stone,
no reason for this greed.

And now I hear, there is a clone,
at a fraction of the cost,
made by machines in factories,
all shiny and embossed.
So should I alter my dream
and settle for a man-made rock,
but first within my own head,
this notion I must unlock.

A good idea I think it is
and I'll certainly be less anxious
knowing the origin of this gem,
no blood on my conscience.
So now it's back to pinching a bit
from my daily expenses,
as I try to curtail my buys
and restructure my finances.
Till then maybe, I'll research all this
just a wee bit more,
So when the time comes to go out and buy,
I'll really be very sure.

Between a Rock and a Very Hard Place

The story of Life
is not one of gentle grace,
but of being stuck
between a rock
and a very hard place.

The romanticism
of a gentle breeze
and the slow lull of waves
exists only in a poet's fantasy
and unspoken craves.

Dewy grass, fragrant flowers,
their beauty,
we sometimes see,
but it's the challenges of Life
that occupy our time
and that's the reality.

Love can be so gentle,
a warm summer embrace,
a heady feeling
of suspension
in an infinite space.

The lightness of being
in a soft floating cloud,
till the euphoric bubble bursts
exposing a nakedness,
from that very shroud.

The joy of sweet surrender
turns into a nagging pain.
The stars lose their brightness
as we doggedly question
our purpose again.

Promises made, dreams shared,
a sense of belonging,
long days, sleepless nights,
the helplessness of longing.

Tides turn,
the waves crash,
a tsunami's on its way
with fury riding piggyback,
washing everything away.

Despondent, broken,
thrust against a rock,
yearning for the comfort,
of silky sand
awaiting the aftershock.

Life floats by
like debris after a storm,
piecing together
random bits,
old memories to transform.

The soul is scarred,
slow is the pace,
yet who can erase
experiences of a Life lived
between a rock,
and a very hard place.

The Dragon

I saw a dragon in the lawn
as I sleep-walked in the early morn.

Was I awake or was I asleep,
I wasn't sure, but I continued to peep.

Through the curtains and the window too,
I definitely could smell the fresh morning dew.

The dragon was long and it was green,
it wasn't fat, nor was it lean.

I think its tail was very long,
it looked so big and oh so strong.

I saw it breathe fire, it was so hot,
I jumped back, away from the spot.

Back into my cosy bed,
chasing crazy images from my head.

And then when I finally awoke,
the alarm bell jolting me like a sharp poke.

I rushed to the window and what do I see?
A sleepy little lizard staring back at me.

In the Mood for Food

I sometimes eat because I'm hungry,
and sometimes it's just sheer greed.
Maybe it's just out of boredom,
or am I fulfilling some latent need?

I'm sure I know the damage,
those nasty carbs can do.
Yet it's the bread basket I attack,
while waiting for my stew.

I plan to start each day healthy,
with breakfast as an important meal,
but soon that bowl of oatmeal
just loses its appeal.

Then it's over to toast and butter
that grace my plate,
and a cheesy omelette is one
to which I totally relate.

A glass of chilled orange juice
pleases me a lot,
along with a slice of creamy cheese,
which I almost forgot.

And some sweetened muesli,
a large bowl if you please,
just leaving place on my plate,
for a muffin on it to squeeze.

And for a beverage to end my meal,
a cappuccino is a must.
Then why am I still hungry,
is a point to be discussed.

I wait an hour, do some work,
my mind to divert,
but unfortunately, to my next meal,
my thoughts continue to revert.

A bar of chocolate beckons me,
as does a pack of crisps,
I look for the jar of salsa
to eat with those yummy chips.

I still have two hours to go,
before it's time for lunch.
So if I eat a mini-meal now,
I guess I could call it brunch.

And with my thoughts so food-obsessed,
and reality unrelentingly keeping pace,
it's no wonder that I've already lost
the 'I'm-trying-to-lose-weight' race!

The Exercise Plan

I'm awake and about
but not in a gymming mood,
desperately trying my thoughts
to turn away from food.

So, while poetry I write,
I wish the flab I could fight,
with the power of my mind,
and not physical might.

But despite trying hard,
my butt refuses to budge,
leaving me dense and heavy,
like a piece of chocolate fudge.

I keep downloading diets,
with weight-loss on my mind,
alas, in this endeavour,
the gods are not being kind.

The cookie-jar entices me,
as the fruit basket looks away,
I guess the start of my diet
will have to wait another day.

The treadmill stands solid
in the middle of my room,
waiting for my footsteps,
and exercise to resume.

I read articles on good health,
and how to keep myself fit,
but then I eat that piece of cake,
and shamelessly continue to sit.

My friends try their best
to lure me off my seat,
I listen very patiently,
then back to my chair retreat.

I even bought a pedometer
to track my daily strides,
but the dismal figures
made me quickly put it aside.

I tried walking up the stairs
till out of breath was I,
collapsing on my comfy bed,
my body, refusing to comply.

I even took out from hiding,
my favourite pair of jeans,
hoping into them to squeeze,
by fair or foul means.

I thought that this would be
the ultimate convincing test,
but my body's resistance,
even won this contest.

So here I am again,
trying new plans to make
and this lethargy and inertia,
from my mind and body to shake.

But surely as we all know,
that's easier said than done,
and though it's a losing battle,
one day it shall be won.

Random Thoughts

Till the rhymes again begin to chime,
it's random thoughts at play,
as I turn my head to make it bend
and look for things to say.

My head is full of many thoughts,
each leaping ahead frog-like,
but the only images that burst forth
are fat, frumpy and such-like.

I wonder how I reached this stage,
and couldn't put my fingers to rest,
as fattening food filled my mouth,
while I struggled to look my best.

Each year I promise myself,
I'll shake the kilos off soon,
but then before I do the deed
I've already reached the next moon.

So bear with me, my dear friends,
as I ramble-tumble along,
and hopefully before the new day dawns,
the koel will have found her song.

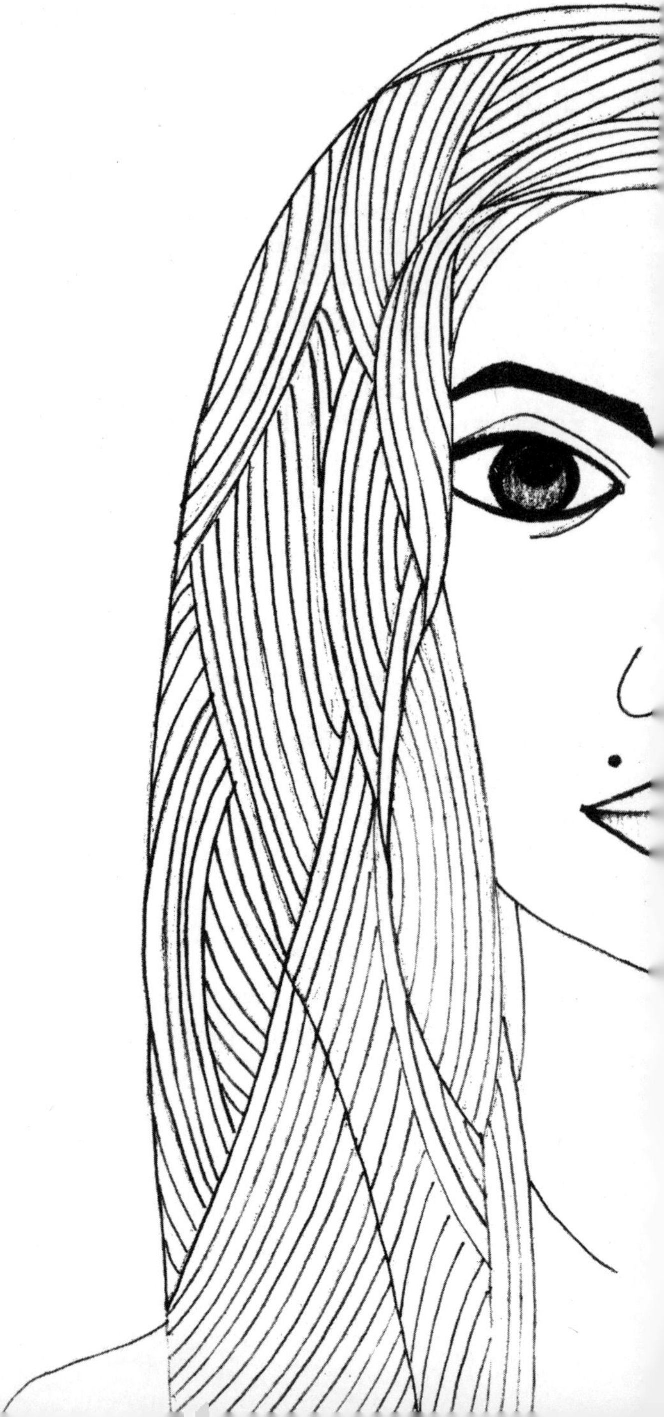

11

Frivolous & Fun

Tommy the Cat

Tommy the cat was a handsome brat
and he loved his beauty sleep,
so if you dared disturb him,
when with food you did lure him,
he'd jump right into your lap.

He was lazy and fat
and loved his cat-nap,
so what if through the day it did extend.
He knew that you loved him
and purred when you pet him,
but never to your desires did he bend.

He was stubborn but smart
and almost like an art,
your heartstrings, he knew how to tug.
By mewing and purring and rubbing and stirring,
when in your bed, you were cosy and snug.

And to shoo him away,
if ever you did try,
he'd give you a defiant stare.
With eyes that glowed brightly
and a tail that perked sprightly,
to show you, he really didn't care.

But, if you went out,
or gave him a shout,
he'd sit by your door and just look.

Till you relented and sometimes repented,
for dear Tommy was a smart little crook.

But, despite all this
and his occasional hiss,
he always was such a dear.
To love and to hold,
to be strong and be bold,
for as a friend he was always near!

Mosquito, Mosquito

Mosquito, mosquito, why are you after my blood
how have you survived the ravages, of even every flood?

An eternal menace, you continue to be
omnipresent, though when I search, you hide from me.

You silently sneak into places and hide
appearing in large numbers, around my bedside.

I think I've got you cornered and turn off the light
but your incessant droning, just adds to my plight.

You've disturbed my sleep for many a night
as you continue to give me a really itchy bite.

I hate you little mosquito, you're an irritating pest
how I wish I could put your entire breed to rest.

I clean up my home to keep you away
yet somehow to enter, you always find a way.

I burn mosquito coils and even use a spray
all through the night and right through the day.

But you little mosquito, are a sneaky pest
hiding in places I can't even guess.

I use every repellent that I can find
but you continue to survive and put me in a bind.

I close every window and quickly shut the door
and when I look around, I see you no more.

But just when I believe that you are finally gone,
I see your family buzzing around the john.

In frustration, I swing my electric bat,
aha, I got you, you pesky little gnat.

And now that I know which weapon works the best
I shall make you my daily conquest.

And annihilate you, even if it's only one by one,
I shall not rest, till this job is done!

Acknowledgements

So many near and dear ones have helped me on this journey of writing and releasing my first book of poems.

My sincere and heartfelt thanks to Shabana Azmi, a dynamic, strong, talented lady, actor par excellence and a great supporter of women's issues, who has so generously and graciously written the Foreword for *The Soulful Seeker*. With poetry surrounding her very being, I couldn't have asked for anyone better! I'm truly grateful for her support.

Chronologically, it all started with a flurry of emails exchanged between school friends from across the world, as we reconnected with one another and the goings-on in each of our lives. Every morning was a delight to wake up to many, many interesting mails and replies flying across with equal speed and enthusiasm. And somehow, even before I knew it, I was writing and replying in rhyme and getting applauded for that. Poetic replies from a few friends made it even more fun and as they encouraged me. I was inspired to start writing poetry beyond just the emails.

More often than not, my daughter Rhea was my first sounding board, and her approval meant a lot to me. My husband Sabbas was next in line and had to patiently listen to and approve of my writing, in the wee hours of the morning, when he got home. My son Rohan, who has been away at college in the US for the past few years, luckily escaped my frequent need for approval. (Sabbas and Rhea also helped me categorise my poems into meaningful sections.)

Various groups of friends, from near and afar, including my brother Vik and his wife Vidya, were targeted next, to read and respond to my rhyming outpourings. They too responded immediately with appreciation. As did my parents, Rajni and Mohindra Chadha, who have always been my first and constant motivators, for every new task that I have ever undertaken. They have always played the most important role in my life!

And so my journey continued ...

As time went by and my collection of poems grew, everyone who cared, started not just encouraging, but in fact almost pushing me into compiling all my ramblings into a book.

Then my publisher Ajay Mago, walked into my life. After hearing me read out just a couple of my poems, he gave me the green signal. It was a very special moment for me.

Dipa Chaudhuri, my editor and I connected almost immediately over cappuccinos (personally made and served by Ajay in his office) and lunch. She, along with my family and friends, once again encouraged me as I started sketching – a new hobby. The result is gently strewn across the pages of *The Soulful Seeker* and on its cover.

As is apparent, a lot of 'encouragement' has helped *The Soulful Seeker* come alive.

To all of you, my sincere gratitude and thanks. May you continue holding my hand forever ...

Punam Chadha-Joseph
Mumbai
January 2016